Victor Rand

ISBN-13: 978-1-937677-80-0
Library of Congress Control Number: 2014939058

Fomite
58 Peru Street
Burlington, VT 05401
www.fomitepress.com

Victor Rand

David Brizer

Fomite

Burlington, VT

To: Lemme Caution
Laszlo Kovacs
J. L. Godard
J.-K. Huysmans

Contents

Acknowledgements

This book, and Victor Rand, would not be here today without the love and inspired encouragement ("Stay strong!") of these, my guardian angels:

Alexandra David-Neel;

Franz Bardon; Violet Firth;

Sophia Beaudine; Charlotte Rampling;

Witold Gombrowicz; Bruno Schultz;

Marc Estrin and Donna Bister; Alex Brizer;

Eliphas Levi;

& to the Shaman of Defiance,

Wherever He or She May Roam

Stella Brizer

Sharon

G. Vintas

CHAPTER 1

TED WILLIAMS

1941 WAS A KILLER YEAR FOR BASEBALL GREAT TED WILLIAMS. This was the year Ted batted .406. What's more, over the course of his brilliant career, Williams hit 521 homers and 1839 RBIs.

We may not have heard the last of him.

Right now Williams is hanging head down in a metal tank filled with liquid nitrogen, in a warehouse somewhere southeast of Scottsdale, Arizona. Waiting for the day when science can thaw him out and make him whole again.

The superstar athlete doesn't lack for company. Other 'suspended' notables include the comic Dick Clair, and an avant garde writer formerly known as FM2030.

Two of every three residents at the cryogenics institute are heads. Just heads. Since it is unclear whether the entire body will (someday, somehow) be needed for revival, prior to death some choose the less costly 'neuro' (=beheading) route. The procedure involves surgical removal of the head followed by immediate immersion in the ultra cool liquid nitrogen bath. (For those interested, the institute is also willing—for a price—to preserve other selected body parts, including strands of DNA).

Prior to deep freeze, the newly deceased body is packed in ice. Within hours (but who's counting, really?) the body is then transferred to a vat of liquid nitrogen, which jams the core temp down to a breezy -320 degrees Fahrenheit. Suspended animation! The kind of stuff you used to read about in books! Various chemicals, preservatives, fixatives and sundry reagents are thrown into the mix. Heparin helps prevent further clotting, and glycerol—anti-freeze—is then added to prevent ice formation and tissue cracking. Cryoprotectant. These life-suspending agents are instilled through a peripheral vein or actually perfused into the heart itself.

Some, especially cryo- and cryonanobiologists, are concerned. With reason. They are concerned that current techniques cannot prevent irreversible damage to the billions of tiny frozen cells. An alternative method, hardly more feasible, involves freeze-drying the body into a block of glass. Vitrification. No muss, no fuss.

Cryogenic societies and enthusiasts have sprung up like wild mushrooms after a heavy rain. Institutes in Grosse Pointe, Death Valley, and Westport, Connecticut are on the cutting edge of this radical new technology.

Goodbye heaven, hello cryonics! Cryonics as a field got launched with the publication of 'The Prospect of Immortality', by Dr. Robert C.W. Ettinger.

Life extenders are ready and waiting to snatch wannabe dust from the mouth of the grave. The key to cryogenic success is ischemia (lack of oxygen) reduction. Vital organs and organelles must be protected from drying out. Tissue viability is maximized by measures including attempts at resuscitation, chest compression, and even Heimlich maneuvers. Those unfortunate enough to revive during such heroic measures are then given liberal amounts of muscle relaxants and nerve poison to prevent the horror of a fully conscious freeze.

At some point the blood is washed out and replaced with embalming fluid. The real key to cryosuccess is timing. Getting to the body as quickly as possible minimizes tissue 'warm time' and cell death. At the warehouse, bodies (or heads, removed *en bloc)* are vitrified or placed in permanent deep freeze.

Golgotha. The Passion of Christ. Suspended in liquid nitrogen.

Does a body thus suspended have a suspended soul, too—a soul that would otherwise be in transit to heaven, to other worlds, or on its way to rebirth?

What would Ted say?

Chapter 2

Kathmandu

A terrible keening, matched only by the incessant howling of the wind, rose among the half-naked monks. What was left of their robes (stiffened for hours by the glacial frost permeating the prayer hut) crackled as they shuffled tirelessly in place in order to keep warm. Their nourishment? Prayer. Their prayer was endless, remorseless, a fruitless caterwauling that stoked the flame of their desperation—yet achieved little else.

Elsewhere on the planet, the Dalai Lama, their Dalai, was at that very moment in spiritual transit from one body—one physical incarnation—to the next. But he was trapped. The physical envelope that housed their master—like the near frozen bodies of the permafrosted monks—was nearly but not quite dead. His Holiness's soul was stuck. His soul could not move on.

Shanduur, chief among the monkish brethren, raised a withered arm. A gesture rife with meaning. The monks fell silent. At once an enormous bellowing rose up among the villages below.

Rajeef, an elder Brother whose lamentations had ceased sometime shortly before, silently fell over where he stood, crumpling into an entropic heap of rags and inanimate frost.

The prayer for the Master's return, the rage of Spirit denied, began anew. Shanduur motioned to his lieutenants in prayer.

Without a sound, without further ceremony, they dragged the fallen monk's inert body and heaved it straight into the crackling hearth. A rank and steady steam slowly rose. First the vestments, then the limbs, then ultimately the trunk and head of the holy man turned to smoke.

Screams, abjurations, untrammeled clouds of woe flew from the icicled throats of the throng. The corpse's vapor would yield a sign, some etheric schemata, which would spell out a plan for the transmigration of the Dalai's paralyzed soul.

Chapter 3

Nice Family Drive

The family was eating Kentucky Fried. The family was eating in the car, with the exception of the teenage daughter who is and had always been a strict vegan.

The family roadster moved along at a nice clip – as smoothly as the breaded chicken wings tumbling into the abyss of their respective bellies. Now the plot thickens, taking on a distinctly unpleasant turn.

The 18-wheeler appeared—seemed to appear—out of nowhere, slamming the Volvo like a gnat into a solid brick wall.

Except the wall wasn't made of brick. (Not that it mattered.) It was made of stone.

Too sudden for words, things happened. No squeaks, no shrieks, not a blink's moment of warning.

One instant a happy family. The very next–smashed, crushed, totaled. Smithereens? Smithereens was just the right word.

But this was not a matter for crossword puzzle enthusiasts. No, not at all. Pomerantz, the dad, makes it. He's alive. 'Alive.' So does Pomerantz's wife, but neither knows it yet. Something wet and warm runs down dad's collar. The windshield, once the proud platform for timely motor vehicle inspections and parking garage permits is now a spider web woven by an arachnid on

LSD. A piece of the canyon, small but deadly, penetrates the once intact glass, in the process impaling the daughter in the cruel and remorseless way nature always seems to have. The Pomerantz girl is now geologic. She has stone befriending and growing into her eye.

THE FOG is in his head, nowhere else. There is vapor, a horrifying clot of smoke, then for Pomerantz there is only dark; then the unmerciful light. What doesn't change is the rank smell. Is it blood? Puke? Has Pomerantz shit himself? His awareness of events comes and goes, like a kaleidoscope that also gives pain. Finally, Pomerantz remembers to flail at the seatbelt, but still he is pinned down, anchored: he cannot move. Pain? Way down just now on the list of bursting impossible priorities. Like the daughter, like the unconscious wife, Pomerantz is transfixed. There are no screams. All he can hear is a wheel, something spinning back there: spinning, smoking and utterly useless. Gail is no longer breathing. Then come the troopers. Sirens, crazy red and blue lights, the heavens splitting open and raining hell upon this most unlucky quondam normative family.

THERE'S MORE. In another part of this particular hell, there are doctors, officials, whatever, guiding the pen in Pomerantz's withering hand. Sir! Sign this. It's your daughter's only chance!

Chapter 4

Decanting

Except for the mosquito bite-sized nick over the eye, the girl is perfect. Not only perfect, but perfectly intact. For all intents and purposes comatose—comatose, but perfectly intact.

Like all the others, she arrives at the cryogenic plant in full regalia—body bag, ice packs and half a hundred shipping labels that obscurely hint at the human freight inside.

Next: Victor Rand. Rand's sleep is shattered by the phone. In what seems like the blink of a (living, working) eye, technician Rand stands before his evening's work. This slim and blonde American beauty is his prize. The decanting team—Joe and Rico, dressed like Victor in street clothes (except for the fashionable dip of their jeans just below the crack of the ass)—heave the parcel onto the table. Moribund parcel? The stainless steel is at least as cold as the beautiful pageant-class babe lying before them.

Rico unzips the tuxedo bag. Without further ceremony (classic poker face included) he rummages, he feels about among the contents. Access: Rico lifts the girl to a position somewhere between semi-slump and semi-upright. Ice packs, sliding from the table and the body of the bluish girl in his gloved hands, crash to the floor in a clinical crescendo that is brief, wordless, yet completely routine.

Now it is Rand's turn. Like the steppe-dwelling monks halfway round the globe, Rand too is frozen.

"Poindexter," Rico bellows. "Snap out of it, man!"

Right. Rand should be turning dials, tickling rheostats, adjusting things. No way on earth he should be paralyzed like this.

Something else is going on. What the hell is it? There's something timeless about the girl. Like he knows her from before. What was this, deja-vu or something?

Rand tears himself free from these thoughts as he reaches for the anal probe. Always the professional, he records the girl's core temperature (Rand was only doing his job; what purpose the procedure served had always escaped him, unless it was a way to hike the family's bill or to somehow titillate a trustees' necrophilia), then prepares the propped-up girl for immersion.

Pity, he thought. Minus the dry cleaner bag, the girl (perhaps those of a more monkish cast would have thought 'the physical envelope' rather more suitable than 'the girl'—whatever—) the physical envelope was stunning…Suspended within it lay one more trapped soul.

Chapter 5

Cry for the Dalai

THE INNER STATE OF THE MONK SAKHALIN IS NOW VACANT, vaporous, tenuous, tenebrous: Sanskrit hell! His eyes lock in mortal/spiritual combat with the equally fierce glaring orbs of Arjuna, his brother in sanctity.

"The wise straw bends with the wind," Sakhalin says.

"There is no wind," Arjuna replies.

Arjuna is older; Arjuna is the more temperate of the two. Arjuna explains that pain—even grief of such profound depth as theirs—is but illusion. There was nothing (literally, 'no-thing') between the two. The junior monk, in other words, was preaching to the choir. Nothing could set them at odds.

The monks agree. The soul of the next Dalai, halted somewhere in transit between its last physical incarnation and the next, had to be set free. Liberated and free to move on. For now the nascent soul, the holy soul, is trapped, trammeled in the perma-frost body of an American girl whose name is Gail. Communal knowledge of this, even among this powerhouse of spiritual adepts, can not on its own thaw the perilous freeze.

Yanno (Yanno the Portly, to his peers) is already quadruped on hands and knees. Yanno dabs glibly at the accessible ice chips melting and dripping from the frozen coruscations of the robe's sleeve.

Arjuna stands, making the perfunctory bow.

"The Young One--they call him Randdh—he already knows."

Sakhalin wonders at this. Sakhalin in puzzled. How can the Young One know? By what means had he learned of this? Deep in the Himalayas there was no Apple store, no cutting edge technology, that could transmit information so fast. Even Sakhalin knew that.

The monks shuffle in place. By rote, by hard won mind control, they suppress the shivers and stamping of the feet that might otherwise distract them from the spiritual task at hand. The hems of their cassocks kiss the puddles at their feet.

"Did he learn by dream? By oracle, by meditation?" Arjuna asks.

"No, foolish one! I called him," Sakhalin says "Even Nosferatu used a cell phone."

MEDICALLY he has no problem with it. Scientifically he has no problem with it.

Victor Rand knows that no human freeze pop could ever hope to survive the killing thaw. Their cells, the heavenly microcosm of their brain circuitry, the circulatory networks, would be irreparably and irreversibly damaged. Some of the bodies on his watch routinely sustained minor (or even massive) trauma to vital body organs. It would be many years before medical technology—or perhaps as yet unheard of technologies—could even contemplate let alone repair this kind of pan-systemic subcellular damage.

Rand hefts the wire cutter in his dominant hand. Odd, how one snip could forever end the possibility—no matter how remote—of this girl's return to life. Subtract the power grid, the crazy spaghetti of cable, silicon, and thermistors, and the liquid nitrogen pump would fall silent, grinding to a fatal halt. It did not matter how lovely the girl was. Beautiful or not, her amniotic bath would thaw, her beautiful organs and cells one by one reverting to their primeval state. Entropy: carbon, hydrogen, nitrogen, and oxygen. The end of the line. One snip of the pliers and the Holy One's Soul—the Dalai Lama's soul—could move on.

He applies the tool to the spaghetti wire ball. The red, blue and yellow strands—one in particular, a cross-hatched blue one—stare at him in unintelligible profusion. Not a time to have fettucini on his mind.

"'Hold it right there, shithead.'"

Too late. The virgin copper at the wire's core appears; then it is cut. The swirling nitro goes dead. Then a larger silence seems to reign.

Rico, furious at Rand's defiant (if not downright insane) act—Rico always had it in for the techie—jumps the smaller man.

Rand topples beneath the weight.

RICO'S MOVE is practiced. (He spends his off hours training at the gym, procuring growth hormones and anabolic steroids until his wallet runs dry. In his time Rico has yanked more heads, broken more necks, than he cares to recall.) Rico grabs the nanotechnologist by the scruff of the neck, jerking Rand up and down, back and forth, with far too much G-force for technician Rand's good...

Searing bolts of pain. Rand feels this. Then come the stars. Actual twinkling stars. Rico slams the boy's skull into the unyielding metal of the freeze tank. One, twice, three times: Rand is out. Stars, comets, then blackness.

Wasting no time, Rico grabs the nearest phone at hand. Not even for a moment does he relinquish his stranglehold on the now very unconscious Rand.

Finally the shop steward arrives. His idea seems ingenious—not just to him, but to his superiors as well. Count on it: the boss always knew what to do. The solution—the only solution, really—was brilliant. They would disappear the kid. Disappear him without a trace...

VICTOR RAND (as he later realized) was never really alone. By the third and final head smash, Rand's ancestral spirit Shaitan appears. Shaitan is very real: a terrible and ferocious warrior—even by the stringent standards of the spirit realm.

Now he is more than real. Thick smoke trails from his ancient habit like rabid confetti, like puce-colored serpents hissing and snapping with rage, with the desperate appetite of the forever damned. The apparition fills the room with its confusion, with the camouflage of its voracious, twisting, Procrustean presence.

A TERRIBLE WAIL, the terrible collective keening of a people faced with imminent doom, rises up from the throng of mountain folk.

Half a world away, Shaitain's turbocharged glance sends his godson's adversary hurling into the opposite wall. Shaitan's spirit, now made flesh, manifests. Shaitan's thought-forms coalesce into fiery triangles, into devilish half-moons. Each and every letter of that flaming alphabet adheres, branding Rico's skin. Rico is scared. Rico has never known fear—certainly not like this. Rico is no longer the assailant. Now he is the target of cosmic lightning, drawn toward his dazed form. Akimbo, balled up in pain, Rico's terror achieves a bowel-emptying pitch. He punches and kicks at the air pathetically, without effect—he is an insect already pinned tight to some mad collector's mounting board.

Victor Rand collects himself, crawling on hands and knees back, way back—it seems like miles—toward the open lid of the nitrogen sitz bath. The girl, propped up in the tank, sits silent, immobile, the center point of the labyrinth of pain and agony that Rand must negotiate—right now!

The freezing broth bubbles and steams no more. Is it possible? Victor detects a movement, a faint tremor, a hint of life, on Gail's face.

At once a marrow-shattering cry erupts from Rico's (almost inert) form. Rico archs, once again kicks ineffectually at mere air. He convulses, his spine spooning then just as suddenly cracking sharply, as Shaitan's etheric current penetrates, fills, then devastates his bones.

Rico is beyond suffocation. Past the threshold of survival. His life hangs suspended, sits on the proverbial razor's edge for just a moment more, then just as quickly what was once Rico is quashed, jettisoned, hurled in the blink of an eldritch toad's eye into a nether dimension of eternal (and it goes without saying, unimaginable) pain.

Many lifetimes will elapse before Rico can once more receive the option of life, of physical sentience. He will enjoy his return to this realm perhaps as a cockroach, a lowly field mouse, even a horse fly. So it is written.

Shaitan abandons the fallen heap formerly known as Rico, withdrawing from the quondam object of his psychic cannonade.

Rand knows his demon familiar well. Shaitan's astral lieutenants are there, hovering, presiding over the clean up of bones and flesh, of the dead meat of this incarnate mess. Rico's earthly remains—clothes, condoms, a disposable lighter, the faintest sprinkling of bone matter—evaporate. Poof! Gone to another more difficult realm.

Stentorian tones fill the icy chamber.

"My son," Shaitan begins.

"I'm not your son," says Victor Rand.

"This is no time to quibble!"

❅ ❅ ❅ ❅ ❅

GAIL IS ALIVE! Warm and alive. She is stark naked, too. Gail sits up, blinks, whisking an errant nitrogen bubble from her (now miraculously intact) eye.

Arjuna: 'Kiss the bride. The next Dalai waits to be born. The dharma is written: The World Master will be your son.'

Rand winks. "Got it, nunc.'

Rand holds the shivering girl in his arms. Despite the ice, she is soft, a beautiful thing. She yields, for certain this time, to his touch. Rand touches his lips to hers.

Shaitan mumbled something, some arcane mantra from a remote corner of his personal galaxy: something about cigars, about registering at Tiffany.

Victor's mouth on Gail's. Two sets of innocent lips.

Gail's soul now his own.

Victor breaks the cinematic embrace.

"This is between me, my girl"—he beams at the naked girl—

the naked goddess—"and the Dalai-to be. Take a walk, old man. And can someone for Siddhartha's sake get me a towel?"

The couple plunge into supernal bliss.

✵ ✵ ✵ ✵ ✵

HIGH in the Himalayan fastness, the Spirit Masters reconvene. It is certain: not only would the Dalai's latest incarnation survive, but it would frigging thrive! Dressed in war vestments—water buffalo skins, frozen lily pads, unfurled prayer flags—the council of Elders locate Gail and her white knight Victor Randdh—now Victor Rand—in the very thick of American suburban life.

Victor and Gail Rachel Rand, of Wilton, Connecticut: living exemplars of bourgeois, decadent, breezy American life. When the time is right, the Tibetan masters will see to every detail. The Rand child—the avatar will be a boy—is destined for Greatness: the perfect life, a perfect home, perfect teachers, perfect spiritual guides. Gail and Victor's son will take his rightful place as the 232nd incarnation of His Holiness, the Dalai Lama. He will teach the world to be happy. Not only that: everyone will stop smoking, too! All will be right with the world.

Chapter 6

Gail's Father

At home, in the playground, in the scrap heaps of abandoned sweat shops, the other kids were just being kids. Not Zach. Zach was already foraging, picking among the herring scraps in the alleyway. Anything for dinner! Barchas, the shop owner, the barrel-chested shop owner with the rivers of dried blood and rendered fat on this butcher's smock, throws him a sour ball or two on the high holy days. Otherwise it is strictly each kid for himself—catch as catch can.

Zach was nine years old and didn't have a heck of a lot of time on his hands. No ringolevio for little Zach. Zach didn't have much time for stickball nor did he have the spare hours or change for movies. No funny papers, no Sunday afternoon at the fireside, no radio thrillers in this little man's dreary life. A few times he tried to cry the situation away; that got him nowhere, nothing—unless you consider the hickory switch and a sore bum as treasures worth something. Afterwards, he would backhand the remaining snot, and sit down to the tense, wordless dinner.

Momma: big and lumbering, a healthy yet miserable creature who makes an art of bestowing her windfall of sorrow on her loved ones and anyone else within range, anyone who would listen. Talk about a captive audience! She smelled funny, too.

Maybe it was the broadcloth dress, worn through over the years to an obscene gossamer sheen. The garment served multiple ends. The shiny smock is what she wears to cook, to work, and to slumber in. The gunmetal iridescence of her knee highs have little to do with silk.

"Zach, your dad has something to tell you," Her breath tainted by sugar diabetes, smelly momma turns away.

"Zachie boy", the old man starts. "Gosh darn it, listen to me when I talk!"

Boy Zach's tumbler crashes to the floor. The drop of milk, no larger than your standard Buffalo nickel, could well have been a puddle of angel's tears.

"We're shipping you out, boy."

"Me? Why me? Where to? And...what did I do?"

Zach is going to Tulsa. That is the long and short of it. Later, much later, Zach will go on to glorify this chapter of his life. He will blather on endlessly about his personal charm, about his magnetism, about his uncanny ability to befriend everyone he met. Everyone, Zach will say, was his friend. ('I never met a man I didn't like,' etc. You know the drill.) Boy Zach, no longer a child, joins the armed forces and is welcomed as a hero (the listener keeps nodding in approval, the trance of approbation worse than a toothache, worse than the listener's own death knell) in every port of call.

After extreme and protracted courtship, Zach's sweetheart, his future wife, future life, and latter-day Procrustean bed, falls for soldier Zach. On V-E day Zach sends her roses, nylons, along with a half dozen packs of Juicy Fruit gum. Zach has survived the war. Flyboy is back home, palming hand-copied poems and half a dozen packs of Juicy Fruit. Things don't get much better than that, now, do they? He was older than she, and he talks like it is going out of style. At least he had a job. He loves the job. Everything he can touch is magicked, entreprenured, enchanted. Ultimately Zach becomes the Septic Tank King of north/north central Enn-Jay— New Jersey to you.

Zach moves his family to an anonymous burb. Few will admit they know the place; the town, Nookencranny, is a 6 point font comma, even on the aerial maps once so dear to the war hero's heart.

Chapter 7

I, Victor Rand

One thing I'll say for Gail Rachel: hers was a terrific rack, a pair of boobs that for me were home: soft, inviting plumped up pillows with the initials 'VR' monogrammed across each. Even more so under that white cashmere sweater she seemed to favor whenever we went out. What made the chemistry so fierce? Was it the rush job--Gail Rachel sweeping me in and out of the center hall colonial before you could say 'Boo!'--or was it the superb fellatio Gail Rachel practiced, that Jewish mouth working overtime in the locked bathroom of the Pomerantz' Nookencranny manse?

I closed the book on Gail's dad Zach with a spadeful of dirt. Zach was gone. I contemplate his death. Chewing my cheeks, I walk away from a barometric reading at the wharf. Suddenly, the whole thing--life, death, what comes in between--seems quite pointless.

Alone at the proverbial helm, I contemplate two issues of burning personal interest: the loneliness of the atom and the certainty of death.

One of Zach's eulogists had said,

'Your good deeds are all you leave behind.' If they could say that about Zach (who had been in retail, a seller of previously owned septic tanks), what would the main sentiment have been at the interment of Michaelangelo, Einstein, Luther Burbank? Whatever happens to the narcissistic rage of the mediocre? What forms do the tantrums if the chronically mediocre assume?

Then it hits me. These religions, these erstwhile sources of comfort at life's great transition points--were vapid, arbitrary, pointless. Only pussy would do.

Speaking of pussy: an old flame of mine makes a habit of dropping in on me at the most unexpected times, leading to a predictable exchange of words and a seduction that always leaves me wanting more. I refer here to Donna, Primadonna née Quisling, the ex-wife who comes to me dressed up as Scheherazade, offering powders and potions as well as her body delectably visible though a floor length black evening gown. 'Take me, darling,' she says. I've had girls chase me, I've had cover girls nymphomaniacs, soap opera actresses who could pirouette at the precise moment of le petit mort...when they 'came'...but it was and never will be enough.

❄ ❄ ❄ ❄ ❄

How many pets, on the other hand, have had the misfortune of watching their owners hang themselves?

The atom cries out for solace but it is too busy with its work. Dancing juggernaut particles, prancing in three non-Newtonian orbits at once.

The lonely atom cries, Is that all there is? Yet the particle keeps at its work keeping at its thankless task—a sub-atomic hero!— of circumnavigating the protons, the neutrons, quantum leaping what seems to him the epicenter, the Alpha and Omega, of its tiny yet vast cosmos. What about fusion? Anyone tell him about that?

With that tart Helen of Troy (yet another girlfriend en passante) I stride the peaks of Parnassus, a phalanx of harpies on my left, their wings beating a grave tattoo of heavenly feathers upon the clouds. I lash myself to the forlorn mast of memory.

Getting back to Zach: why do I say, Zach broke my heart?

Wow, I thought, Gail Rachel's knee sandwiched between mine. Not only is she stacked, but she comes with lots of baggage too: the Pomerantz' lawn, graced by the very best septic tank money can buy...Gail's family was solid, solid as rock: they had beliefs, they cared, they belonged!

I believe I am firmly clasped to the ample bison of this family.

And every moment on the Turnpike, every spine-jarring second on the Amtrak, brings me closer to her, to her furry and pulsing and soft brown nucleus.

As Zach ages, accumulates the invariable infirmities and pardonable deficits of the elderly, my life with Gail takes a nose dive. My bitterness grows by leaps and bounds. Each night I am at the office later and later.

My grief does circus acts, high wire flips, executes impossible leaps through hoops of fire. No more stops at the sweet shoppe for chocolate.

I harden my heart. I have to. It occurs to me, the logical terminus of all this suffering: I will end my marriage. I will spurn those life-giving breasts. I will walk alone.

Chapter 8

Emily

"Victor, why the hell can't she just die?"

This was the gorgeous blonde's advice. The very same gorgeous blond who was naked and in my bede. With me! She was also telling me a dream but I didn't or couldn't hear it through the twin eructations of my heart and my groin.

"Yeah Victor: die!"

I met the girl at work. Her look totally goads me on. It was a fusion bomb: wild celibate animals who finally and triumphantly score. She is receptive. On so many levels.

One other minor detail. I, Victor Rand, am her boss. Actually, she works for me. I wasn't (I flatter myself) born yesterday. Of course I foresee a blizzard of problems, litigation tougher and stronger than any dream team could ever concoct. I see calendar pages, endless reels of tabloid newsprint and video-tape, flapping in the wind. I see myself bowing and scraping before wigged and powdered magistrates determined to take me down.

It started the day we met. Over 'coffee.'

"Know about the Bardo?"

Immediately I regret the question...

She plays dumb.

"The Tibetan Book of the Dead. The owner's manual for the soul."

"I don't read manuals. Should I make an exception? Just this once?"

"Well this particular manual was written over two thousand years ago. How to cross over to the Great Beyond—without losing your soul."

She declines the shapeless eggs. Great. She hates manuals and she hates eggs. Eyes like hers don't need eggs.

"Guess what?"

She keeps looking at me, straight and deep into the limpid (tearing? I wonder) pools of my useless eyes.

I see it, plain as day: the two of us tussling, grunting, groaning in bed.

"Black, no sugar, and—thanks."

Where to go next? Stick with the White Light—or move on to Dutch Schultz? In either case she'd be bored beyond reckoning. In less than twenty minutes I finish my soporific diatribe on kabbalah. Anything to impress her. I'm running out of things to say.

"Armagnac?"

"Am I talking too much? Just say the word."

"Go on, please. Somewhere you're hitting a nerve."

Good. The ball was still in my court. Or was she referring to a particularly malevolent migraine?

"I know: tennis. You and me and the clay court in between."

"Yes."

Fuck the Bardo. Fuck the afterlife. It's about now. It's about...tennis.

How I regret the scrambled eggs, sitting there before her like the steaming innards of something you swerve at all costs to miss.

I felt vulgar, absolutely vulgar, with this girl. I felt like a pig; a prig; a broken twig. An earwig.

I was making love, to her, in the medieval courtly sense. The brains come together then the bodies follow. For the life of me, I could not stop talking.

"Say more."

Like I need an invitation.

These conversations...Good Lord, but they could run on! Somewhere in Brooklyn a butterfly dies. A flamenco player in Madrid is gored by a maddened bull. And so it goes. All over the world people are falling in love.

"Hope you like working here."

The girl shows up for a job, ostensibly breakfasts with the department chair... and gets Diderot, Larousse, and Sanskrit instead. I want to vomit. Truly I do. Instead, I pay the check.

I THINK we conversed. Covering, as they say, a lot of ground. Many sidelong glances, too. We ambled down a long corridor as I fished in my pockets for trinkets, bubble gum, anything to distract myself, to relocate my mind from its neurotic labyrinthine hell.

"Tennis."

"I'll bring my equipment."

So will I, you luscious piece of ass.

Everything in its own proper time.

Later that night, I make conversation, breathless sallies at intelligible speech, each more hysteroid than the last. Big Sol, bestfriendMeister from the Bronx, listens with practiced poise. He is reticent, terse... when I need his boundless loquacity the most.

"Watch out, chief. Oh and by the way—good luck. Later, Maestro."

"Tennis?" I ask.

"Raw and vulnerable."

She does not do things by the book.

I try, cold showers and naked anchovies, but nothing helps. Not thinking about her hurts. The premonition, I think, of a cerebrovascular accident, an unwonted near-fatal stroke.

"Do not, I repeat do not get with her," Big Sol implores.

Right. And the earth was built of whey....

Now we are smooching, seriously at it. Suddenly I come up for air.

I break the kiss. Would she in turn break my heart?

"That dream. Tell me abut that dream."

What's a man to do? Immediately I call upon the spirit of my grandpa— a confirmed horse thief from Russia—to steer me right.

"Why can't she just die?" This time she doesn't smile.

Her dream had two parts. With proper handling, so could Gail's body. Is it the girl? Or too much caffeine, not enough sleep?

I read to her in bed. {Hemingway, not Diderot.} She slips off her clothes. I see her breasts.

The sex part—our very first time together—was dry to start, became juicy, sometimes both. It doesn't matter. I impaled her. She burned sage.

Another (epochal) time we were shopping. Town plaza, upscale shops—the very best!—that kind of thing. Emily chooses a hundred dollar fern as a gift for our friend. She hands the fern to Gene.

"I like your friends…"

"That remains to be seen."

VICTOR, get a grip. I'm akimbo, practically brain-damaged, in bed with this stunning woman who loves me so much. She bought my pal a fern! Already I'm thinking, thinking far too much. Truth to tell, I'm thinking larvae. What it is. What in tarnation we have here. Fever, that's what we have. Two lives shedding wrappers for the serpent power within.

She hands me a cup. No, not exactly: she hands me a silver chalice. Every fucking gesture ripe with meaning. Her mouth, her trim little cunt: snakes swallowing tails, a steeplechase Ouroboros that will rocket me to the heights, plunge my soul into the depths.

Rand (at moments of crisis, he slips into the third person singular. Next stop: talking to myself late at night, down an endless empty street.) Rand distracts her with his wand, supposedly a keepsake of Aleister Crowley's that he picked up at a flea market in south central Jersey for loose change. Blood rites in Oaxaca mean nothing to her, leave Emily clueless, leave Emily cold. Her carnelian eyes widen a bit but that's as far as it goes. Rand knows lust. Rand knows lust: the corners of her eyes, her eyes, her eyebrows. Stop signs turning Aramaic. Everything around Rand turning to gold.

"I'LL DO anything for you," she says.

So we book a flight for a sex club, a den of iniquity for the clean-shaven, somewhere in Benares.

TENNIS? She plays a lackluster set but then again she knew things that would take Rand a lifetime to learn.

HE LEARNED things.

He learned things about her.

They work at a service agency, a long corridor separating the respective offices of the lovebirds.

She reveals herself to him by degrees: carefully, by meridians, ley lines, degrees. A masterful seduction, really; by the time Rand knows it, it is far too late.

She needs to throw herself before the gods. She needs to lap dance Zeus in an Olympian titty bar.

And Victor Rand couldn't tear away. Were Emily's eyes merely mortal? At the agency they steep themselves in the suffering of others. Servicing coils, cables, peristaltic waves of suffering humanity. Men, women, and children at the mercy of dumb luck; at the mercy of those who would deprive them of their niggardly public entitlements.

He loved her lips. She didn't speak much. Poetic license. Suspension of disbelief. Talking to her was like jet-skiing the Styx with a George C. Tilyou smile on his face.

THE MORE he thought about it, the more he loved her.

She wants him to quit the agency.

"Enough suffering."

"Agree."

"The agency sucks. It's a fucking dive."

It was shabby. It's just that he didn't notice how shabby until she started working there.

"We can't be seen in public. Why, we can't even go to the Kabbalah Center together."

Ouch. Wow. That was really hitting below the belt.

THIS WILL CAUSE me pain. Somehow, somewhere, I will surely pay. He wonders if the agency would send him as a delegate—or better yet—as a victim, to a public execution.

'They only do injections now,' she said. 'No more hangings. Gone is the era of the electric chair.'

A vision comes to Rand: in his mind's astigmatic eye he sees bloody burlap sacks filled with freshly guillotined heads. According to eyewitness reports, newly decapitated heads bite and curse each other before succumbing to death. Flailing in extremis, he guessed. Rand prefers to think of his girlfriend, her beautiful head and neck and all the rest of her completely intact. From the margin of mortality (vide infra} he will invoke her face. She will be the most extravagant daisy on the hummock of his grave.

Rand was about to start on Dutch, the Dutch diatribe: it was his favorite of them all. Dutch Schultz...but then he noticed how her taut lips, taut and thin, with a color somewhere between pink and ice blue, drive him wild. The thought of her lips, their otherworldly perfection, of her lips, makes him hard.

I should be writing science fiction, Rand thinks. Or moving to Paramus, at the very least.

Yet another friend cautions him about falling in love.

Rand ponders this, but the well-intentioned comment doesn't rock his world.

"WHAT about tennis?"

Nothing.

"Okay, have it your way: how about sex? Let's have sex."

"Slow down, mister...don't get cute."

MEANTIME...Gail butchers her family. Hacking herself, the dog and the azaleas to kibble-sized pieces. Flailing them alive. Reminds him of a Bengalese restaurant they like, located on the wrong side of town. Either you craved the stuff or you didn't...you tossed.

AFTERNOON at the agency. Everyone but Rand is gone.

Fuck the music of the spheres, Rand thinks. I can never have this girl. And what perverse instinct prompted me to goad her on with that Bardo bullshit?'

One good turn deserves another. Rand awards himself a D-minus in Impression Management. He resolves to place this black mark/pink sheet on the Human Resources desk, first thing in the morning.

HE COULD SMOKE. He would take up smoking. Start with cigars, bidis, water pipes...pick up right where he left off. Trigger an ophthalmoplegic crisis. Tobacco amblyopia. Anything to impress this girl! Fly away on the wings of self-neglect.

CASUALLY, secretly, on the QT, he takes over more of her paper work. Neither Venus de Milo nor Helen of Troy did paperwork. Neither would she. Each time he signs Emily's name a defiant artery throbs like a tiny death knell in his hand. An imperious little throb. Scary? No. Yes! Rand smells fear and death and camphor, truckloads of the stuff, headed his way.

Could he jack off reading Beckett? He is about to try when the phone rings, interrupting his psychosexual daze.

"Can I come over?"

Hell, it was only midnight. Early in the grand scheme of things. Especially with the wife and kids away and countless hours till the frosted glass of the agency doors would be thrown open to welcome that day's quotient of the poor.

"You mean it? Come over here?"

"Yes."

Gosh. Gee willikers, Mrs. Cleaver...

This was it: the big one, the big enchilada. Victor Rand has hooked the marlin. He stammers out directions to the house (already knowing that she already knows), paying out line inch by inch, one hand at a time. Crisis. Action. Grace under pressure. Something out of Hemingway, or Moby Dick. His pulse slows and he mops his fevered brow.

Reel her in.

Reel him in.

Clean up time!

Family photos turned pell-mell to the wall. Dim the lights. Rand jumps in the car.

The lovers meet on a deserted boulevard. A rundown State Farm office on one side of the road, a graveyard (another portent?) on the other. Auspicious, no? Under the sign ('Service Claims Office') she falls into his arms, plunging that delicious *goyische* tongue deep inside his mouth. Their serpent powers entwine, embrace. Catherine wheels flare and die in the still suburban night.

LATER, IN BED, he is complaining again. "Too many words. I can only stand so much."

"Quit your job," she says. "Write science fiction instead."

"I'll never run out of words for you," he says.

"Great,' she says. 'But can you get rid of Gail?"

RAND'S DOG watches: Rand and mistress at play. This couple was all work. The mastiff, unmoving from his guilt-making perch, watches. Eventually there is dawn, there are birds, great fear. Trying to fuck Emily in the bed that Gail Rachel brought home, so many Saturdays ago.

"I can't," she says, gently moving his questing hand from down there up to the more permissible zone, "wrong time of month."

Lunar landscapes, rising tides, Frazier's Golden Bough.

Whatever, Rand thinks. This is the love of my life. In my marital bed. This is the handiwork of the devil.

How would Cotton Mather handle this?

"THIS IS MY HOUSE," Rand explains. (*Not for long*, a cicada chimes in.) Always the gentleman. An excellent if somewhat ambivalent host. She was new at the agency. A new hire. Now she sits in Jesuitical judgment of his cock.

Chapter 9

The Love Song of J. Alfred Hitchcock

How much was she guessing? More to the point, how much does she really know?

Would he end up like the rest of them, a clone, just another face among the mewling crowd standing on line at the agency door? 'I did the time, but I didn't do the crime?'

Am I really a felon? And what about Zach?

Rand's thoughts snap back, ceding his twisted brain—cerebral convolutions, gyri, and all, back to the Here and Now. How many Hitchcock films had she actually seen?

Rand stumbles on (nothing new there!), without a clue.

Double Indemnity. Rand narrates the plot for her, reciting it frame by harrowing frame.

No response.

What does he expect—does he expect her to drool? Decorate him with a garland of hugs?

"We're supposed to have kids. The issue of my loins…The unborn children…will be heartbroken."

"They'll get over it. Kids these days are amazingly resilient. We'll have our own."

"They'll miss her."

"Who? You haven't even knocked her up yet. Don't. Or you can forget about us." *Martinet*, he thinks. *Bitch.*

She leans forward in her cat-like way. A tigress to the core. The tiny golden hairs on her face melt him. His judgment dissolves in thin air: Bye-bye! What a girl! It's not just the sex. It's the tiny blonde hairs on the back of her neck. Whatever he gives she takes to heart. She takes his things into her precious heart, stows them there, slowly but surely accumulating a dime-store collection of all he holds dear.

He's dizzy. Punch drunk. Once he does the job…well, maybe then he'll unwind.

She looks at his feet (this burns him to the quick) and bursts out laughing. Good Lord: your feet are colossal! Humongous! Your feet are so…big!

Did Dutch Schultz's girl mock the mobster's feet? And if she did, what happened next? Did Dutch endure it; laugh it off; or did he give her a good shot in the kisser? Would Rand laugh all the way to the chair?

Things quickly get out of hand. She was born long after the Cold War; East European war games, Ugandan warlords, and Siberian military colleges meant nothing to her. Who is she? What is she really about?

No doubt: his nerves are bad. Bad and getting worse all the time.

He sneaks a bulletin ('Men Who Feel Too Much') from the College of Neuraesthenia into his briefcase.

"They'll miss her," he squeaks (again.) Is he obsessed? What was up with Rand and his unborn tots?

"Get over it. The children will. Or am I talking to the wall?"

The way she snaps at him, the martial tone in her voice, that absolute certainty—all that gets him hard too. Hey, the future Dalai's resilient; His Holiness can take it, if anyone can.

Besides, there is no death penalty in Connecticut. The rest of his life behind bars? The stuff of pure romance.

A friend asks him if the sex is good.

Rand laughs in his face.

To HIS CREDIT, Rand tries separation, even divorce. He and Gail are like the walking dead. History. Herstory. The tension arcs between them like a welder's flame. The flame now a regular feature of any time when they can endure each other's company, one-on-one. Losing that lugubrious silence would tarnish the little they still had. Gail could lapse at any moment into tears or rage or what Rand really hated, a dull and withering stupidity.

Chapter 10

The Big House

Welcome, Bienvenue, Welkommen…Welcome to the club. *Arbeit macht frei!*

Welcome to the diocese of sorrow, to the precinct of tumbrils, to the topsy-turvy gardens and redolent camphor forests of Pluto.

Rand has time on his hands—plenty of it. Lots of time to talk. Self-expression is a mixed blessing in this place. But not too much! Men languish behind bars. Killing as a birthing experience—a New Age hayride, a romp in the park. If Gail survived the attack (Rand doubted she had) she could go to meetings, hook up with the other wives and girlfriends of their abductors, tormentors, shooters.

Get over it.

That's what they keep telling him.

Rand writes withering letters to the editor of obscure jail fanzines. Prisoners' rights, they call it. For example: The separation, he writes, like a violent scission, a coming apart of a common world-view. A world-view which had reigned until that moment when I decided to make myself heard…heard with absolute authority, with a terrible violence that obscures the 'criminal' in 'criminal act' for me. I didn't know I had it in me. And now I am serving time because of some cunt's epidemic sense of right and wrong. A marital bond which reigns supreme over the personal conditions and terms of the coevals. I spend my nights on an iron cot next to a serial bomber, an expert in plastique who dreams of someday donning the mantle of the law.

"ARE WE REALLY beyond hope?" Gail had asked. "Is the marriage really doomed?"

"Everyone else," she continued, "is going on with their stable, peaceful lives." Meanwhile she was convening angry wives' cabals and egregious study groups.

Rand longed for a companion. A pen pal. A study partner. Face it: that girlfriend, that wife, that entire way of life, was over. Who or what could ever take their place?

In prison they encourage Rand, *ad nauseam*, to ventilate his feelings.

True, they couldn't watch certain movies (although rumor had it there was a bootleg copy of *Scarface* floating somewhere around Cell Block 9); but they could write and recite any damn thing they wanted.

THE MARRIAGE got off to a shaky start. I promised Gail we would never part. I clasped her hand as the cab tore me from her side. We raced over the Kosciuscko, away from the city, away from commitments, away from Love.

I called her every night.

She promised to join me soon. (Otherwise I would never have left.)

Months later I was still calling her. Pleading with her from my poured concrete hovel out west. Her words were sweet, like a Balm of Gilead—but still, girl no come! She assured me she would soon be at my side. I made a life for us. Seven months later she appeared, luggage in hand, at my lonely door. I imagined her pregnant, imagined her carrying not just luggage but child, begging to stay.

"Have a drink," she said.

"This is nothing," she said, lowering her eyes, pressing her gravid belly in my daydream against mine. "All that matters is now. Now that we're together."

Right. I should have thrown her out on her estrogen-depleted ass. But I was weak. Immediately I caved, held her in my arms. Soon enough she would carry my child. Murder one would come later. Right then, I was already hard, eager to end the 7 month dry spell.

Word of her adultery had spread. Spread like wildfire. Those in the know could not believe their ears.

"Mothafucka!" they cried. "You been had!"

Gail's response was cool. "Most husbands would look the other way, Victor. Most guys are happy when their wives have close friends."

Chapter 11

The Big House Redux

Tracking the Dwindling Star that Has Been My Life
By inmate #181924

THE UNUSUAL or should I say somewhat foreign-sounding name—
after all, not everyone gets a six digit number for their surname—
belies my very ordinary background, my all too predictable failures
in the twin realms of literature and life (marriage.) Of one thing I
am certain: the double decline, the deadly declensions of marriage
and art of which I shall speak (will ye listen or not!), absolutely
make sense.

Best to begin at the beginning. One chooses an arbitrary point
in time for a launching point. Or adjust if you prefer the tele-
scope's eyepiece, in order to track the dwindling star that has
been my life.

MY FORMER WIFE Gail had many friends. So many attachments,
infatuations, idolatries, idealizations. Granted: I should have
known from the start. Having, gaining, or winning her devotion
was like buying a fraudulent lotto ticket, a junket to the bottom
of a weed-choked sea.

Too caught up in my issues? Am I really? Having barely survived the primitive felicities of my own 'childhood', I managed to steer a course this side of sanity by clinging to some vague and effete notion of self-expression. I thought writing would save me. A published writer penetrates his readers' minds and hearts, like it or not. The exigencies of time, fate (and the horror of a penniless future) await most writers…Exigencies that awaited me, arrangements and future games that eventually derailed and devoured me whole.

Writing? No way. Instead I found work in an agency, incinerated my soul in the 'cure of souls'…squandering my meager energies in the care of the spiritually wounded instead of lancing my buboes, applying carbolic to my own festering sores. (The entry ends here-Editor.)

Visualizing a Healthy Space
By Inmate #181924

I compose these complaints, these wretched ruminations, from the vainglorious aerie of my prison cell. I am in prison somewhere in the florid torrid aptly named state of Florida. I am in exile, separated from my unborn children, from anything even remotely resembling the fulfillment of the smallest part of my dreams. Somewhere out there palm trees list in a tropical breeze. Glib, glib as palms can be. Perhaps a storm is in the offing.

Nowhere is home.

And then, the wracking, insuperable loneliness. A by-product, as it were, of the non-elective mutism that clamps its steely muzzle on many inmates in places such as this.

I am a voyeur, an alien astrally projecting his soul two fathoms above the streets of the tropical town. From on high I watch the parade; smell the stink; hope to torch the absolute effigy of humanity. Sweethearts young and old, it does a body good to think of the ten thousand lips, locked in that unending spectacle of gonadal bliss, all those anthers, stamens and pistils clutching at each other, *in flagrante delicto,* in mindless profligate frenzy... It does a body good, I say...but not mine!

Not me, not my soul wracked by violent antipathies...

Not me, rat-man extraordinaire, spending his useless little time lining his burrow with pathetic leavings, with *objets trouves* and the flotsam of a blasted alternate sworld...

ALL THE ATROCITIES, all the heinous crimes that one can inflict on another (short of murder or the artful application of the garotte) have been committed in the name of marriage...against me.

The actual list of abuses, dear prison doctor, will have you in tears, the utter banality of this catalogue I offer you, its predictability, its unswerving dedication to her mission....The list includes defamation, moral defloration, derogation, slander, libel, verbal abuse, taunting, mockery, belittling, emasculation, character assassination, devaluation of all types, ball-busting, betrayal, desertion, negligence and cruelty of the most primitive banal stripe.

This vituperative harridan, this Wiccan whose ferocity is amplified by a stunning blindness of self—AND MOST ALL BY

THE COMPLETE ABSENCE OF LOVE, COMPASSION, AND KINDNESS—this shrew, this virago, this harpie who should never have ventured beyond the limpid Stygian pools, this expert at neglect—has degraded me, flailed and stripped me of all dignity, has flown into literal rages at the merest pretext, at the drop of a hat...

Chapter 12

Dutch (aka Arthur Flegenheimer) Schultz

Arthur Flegenheimer: The little kid? That's me. Standing proud in my sailor's suit, six flights up. That apartment was a bower, a fucking swatch from the goddamned Unicorn Tapestry…

You want to hear about the Concourse, the Grand Concourse? A bleeding fucking artery in a puking terrain. That was some street! That street ate you, chewed you up and spit you out, digested your dagos, wops and spics—this was democratic digestion, without regard to race, creed or color—digested them whole, them and their smokes rolled up tight in their sleeves… Their wifes shopping, yapping, beating each other down to grab the last piece of crap on sale. Alexander's, the Loew's Paradise, Fordham Road…Remember the monster, the freak who shrieked at the dark windows, led by his poor bind dray? 'I sell old clothes!' He sharpened your knives, a stevedore and his baby carriage, overflowing with rotten junk? They call it good feeling, *gemutlichkeit,* running in rivers, flowing like milk and honey, touching everyone everywhere: the natty dressers, the bums, the babes in arms…The Concourse? October draughts throwing handfuls of dead leaves at you like monsoons, like unhappy hay rides, October draughts tonguing the privates of the turbaned *tantes* on parade, yeah that was some Concourse!

The Grand Concourse. Right. Versailles with a boxwood fringe. Four miles of concrete canyonland. Ten thousand fucking trees, each and every one boiling over with sap—in the Bronx! Oldsmobiles and Buicks running wild, hubcaps and fenders with soft curvy hoods polished like mirrors—like sacred icons, poison votives I tell you, a religious festival at crescendo...

We lived at 1500. 'Lived.' Pop never understood me; he never wanted to! Said I was a mistake. Maybe that's why I was so fucking moody. Hell—#1500 Grand Concourse. A wonder to behold: an art deco piece of shit. The fucking Thin Man should have lived there—not me! Blue glass, pylons, good booze and girls, girls with sheer seamed stockings and garter belts...Big fucking deal.

I spent too much time alone. Too much time in my room. Pain. At the end of the day, that's what I remember most—I remember the pain. I remember lightning bolts coming straight for me. I see the light in the window like someone's war paint and it made me jumpy, makes me want to jump.

They had a name for me. Said I was an oracle: 'Father Time.' Hell, I didn't mind. And I didn't mind the room. The room was fine, painted some 'easy on the eyes' shade of blue. Eggshell blue they call it. The carpet was a battleground for my toy soldiers. Know how Napoleon conquered the world? He mowed his enemies down with a cannon. A fucking cannon. That's right, the carpeting in my room. That's where I planned my moves. I was a kid but I was old enough to plan. Appomattox, Little Big Run...a final resting place for all the enemies still to come...With me in command, they were already stiff in the grave.

INTERVIEWER: Dream archipelagoes heaped and stinking with sun-choked fruit?

ARTHUR FLEGENHEIMER: Fuck you too, Mac. Yeah, I was 'sensitive.' One way or another the shit's got to come out, no? Mind you—I never slept. Tiny bunnies, lambs even, would climb on my face, get caught in my hair. Oh yeah—did I mention the sickbed, the 'unexcused' absences and truancies from school? I always had a cold. *Doe Skin.* Yeah. They stopped making them, probably the same day I learned to jack off. You can't get them anymore.

INTERVIEWER: Their Disney eyes and squirrel tails back-lit by the first approaching rays of dawn?

ARTHUR FLEGENHEIMER: You a fairy, or what? What's that shirt made of? My mom and pop loved me in their own way, loved me the best they knew how. Forget about the crack of dawn. Four a.m, Pop was out of the apartment, gone, hauling boxes of fish. That's why he always stank. Other times, one or two weekend mornings in my entire life, things were different. The dish water running, the eggs and bacon frying—that's right, the Concourse Jews liked bacon too—the folks finally got it right. I can count on the fingers of one hand the number of times I felt welcome in this miserable world. My mom in the kitchen, the running dishwater, my mother *shh*!ing everyone because the *kindeleh*—that's me—was asleep. That's when he whacked her, gave her a good one, a *zetz* they call it, a *zetz* for all time, right across the lip, or upside that noble unstinting head. Then he would have finished her, the fuck. The fuck with his fist tight with fish. No more good dreams for me.

INTERVIEWER: Suddenly-arrived visions, tunnels, the skull-and-crossbones regalia of the netherworld?

ARTHUR FLEGENHEIMER: I'll just make like I didn't hear that, okay? I couldn't keep away from the window, from the drawn blinds. Big night out there. Lots of electricity, lots of power. Big purple sky, what with the neon, the gun shots, the stars dancing with the moon in the heavens above…and all the comets can say is, Fuck you. Have fear. How did I get to be such a tough guy? Gee—I thought you'd never ask! One time I'm a Concourse cowboy, strutting my stuff, avoiding the dog shit and hummocks of tubercular spit. Concrete pampas, you might say. Prairie dogs, coyotes, the kid's imagination going full tilt. I'm a half-pint, dressed to kill. Ten-gallon (ten ounce) hat, silver stirrups, toy gun in holster: you get the picture. I'm bad. Righteous, too. I got the law on my side. Hell, in my imagination, I was the law.

INTERVIEWER: Fleets of shiny Pontiacs—cars, not Indians—tear across the range.

ARTHUR FLEGENHEIMER: You got that one right, chief.

INTERVIEWER: In the near distance, a mesa or two shimmers in the heat.

ARTHUR FLEGENHEIMER: I'm waltzing on the sidewalk, counting the clouds.

INTERVIEWER: Minding your own business, lost in your dreams, when suddenly…you spot him. Leaning against the building. The smelly old vagrant gives you the proverbial evil eye.

Arthur Flegenheimer: The wops call that *Malocchia*. The guy is old. This guy is very old. So damn old it hurts him to breathe. The old fuck waves me over, flagging me down.

Interviewer: Way up, beyond the buildings, an iron bird arcs toward Montana.

Arthur Flegenheimer: I'll pretend I didn't hear that. The guy motions to me. 'Hey kid, look what I got.' The geezer's talking to me. Says his name is Cody. Wild Bill Cody, something like that. 'Ever heard of me?'

Interviewer: Right. Wild Bill Hickock, caught somewhere between rickets and a half-paretic sneer…He sputters then chokes, hawking the whole gob up. Something even the alley cat couldn't keep down.

Arthur Flegenheimer: Somehow he manages to lasso his phlegm. 'Mighty fancy duds, sonny boy,' he goes, 'Had some fine threads myself, one time.'

Interviewer: Wistful.

Arthur Flegenheimer: I couldn't tell if he was going to laugh or cry. "I rode with the best of 'em. Yup." I couldn't take my eyes off him. I had to get closer, take a better look.

INTERVIEWER: As you approach he folds up into himself. A truly impossible position: like a bug, a praying mantis…

ARTHUR FLEGENHEIMER: He knows he's got me. I'm staring now. I'm eating him up with my eyes. Wild Bill is really into this. Him and his damn fool stories got me hooked.

WILD BILL: I sure do remember them, as though they was right here. right now, in their own flesh and blood. Jesse James. Wyatt Earp. Billy the Kid. Now that Jesse—that was one mean fella. He'd as soon buy you a drink as fill you full of holes. Ventilate you, you know? It was all the same to him. Those were real men sonny. Real men.

INTERVIEWER: You can't help noticing a certain tang creeping into his words.

ARTHUR FLEGENHEIMER: Tang? I'd call it poison. More like poison.

WILD BILL: Living breathing men. Like you and me, right now. My namesake—Wild Bill Hickock to you—stood damn near as close to me as you're standing right now. Breathin' down my neck, fixin' his fine young eye on the horizon, always scoutin', always on the lookout, countin' his ponies, figgerin' how many miles he had to go. how may bullets in his gun…and guess what?

INTERVIEWER (simultaneously):What?

ARTHUR FLEGENHEIMER: (simultaneously): What?

ARTHUR FLEGENHEIMER: He stopped. The old man stopped. He hacks up something, piece of lung or something…I look up brightly, expectantly, waiting for the prize.

INTERVIEWER: You're a child. This is the moment you've been waiting for. The arroyo—I mean the Concourse--is silent as the moon.

ARTHUR FLEGENHEIMER: Even the Pontiacs have ground to a halt.

WILD BILL: Any idea where they all be now, boy? YOU GOT ANY IDEA?…
    They is dead, sonny. Dead. Every last one of 'em.

ARTHUR FLEGENHEIMER: And that's all she wrote. Little Artie's childhood gone forever. Quick and dirty, just like that.

INTERVIEWER: The traffic, the pigeons, the shopping carts grind to a halt…then just as suddenly resume their plowing, flying, driving, like some orchestra from hell.

ARTHUR FLEGENHEIMER: Me? This old wheezer tells me someday I'm gonna die? Me?

INTERVIEWER: But Cody keeps on talking. Like he's discussing the weather, the stock market, the Trifecta…

ARTHUR FLEGENHEIMER: I don't want it. Not this. Hell, I want my mommy.

INTERVIEWER: Like one of those newsreels, on fast forward, You're seeing everything clear, the way it really is, for the very first time. Your friends, your family, reduced to ashes, reduced by the dance of time to dust. Only dust.

ARTHUR FLEGENHEIMER: Too much! I'm seven fucking years old. No matter. Loneliness comes to stay. Twenty minutes before you had a basically normal kid. Now everything was ruined.

INTERVIEWER: Exiled from childhood by the oxygen-starved rantings of a spittle-daubed relic.

ARTHUR FLEGENHEIMER: You can run but you can't hide.

INTERVIEWER: You want, with every ounce of your being, to obliterate Cody's 'revelation.' But it's too late.

ARTHUR FLEGENHEIMER: Instead I run upstairs. That being the first and last time I ever cried.

INTERVIEWER: Wait a sec. Hold up. What was this snaggle-toothed codger doing in the Bronx, anyway?

ARTHUR FLEGENHEIMER: I was too young to ask.

Chapter 13

More Dutch

Dutch grew up 'standard', in an apartment in the Bronx. Some say it was Brooklyn but I know better. The building was important in his life: the building and those who lived in it and the Grand Concourse too: they made him want more. The old ladies schlepping their shopping carts; fighting to the death for the premium cuts of lox, of herring; drooling into the pickle and pot cheese barrels… all this would go on forever, if Dutch had his way. Sure, Dutch's parents were common folk, hewn from the coarsest threads of humanity. Still, to look at them you would never think, This boy is a born killer. He has a future in Kabbalah.

I knew Dutch for a time. I was one of the kids who ran screaming, propelled by a perfect mixture of fear and delight. Kids joyfully lost in the Minotaur's lair: lost in that dark, dank basement, where the mammoth boilers and furnaces perpetually thundered. No doubt about it: this basement was special. The building's nameless 'super' kept an apartment down there—which only frightened us more! What manner of beast was this, this man who walked, unharmed, among the half-formed denizens of the dark? The superintendent's place…seemed to open to still more basement; his lodgings lacked windows. I don't remember the super but I sure as hell remember his dog. Of one thing I was certain: there was a fierceness to the place, some horrid kernel of truth surrounding the legends of those who had wandered too far in to ever return to the diocese of light.

Killer instinct? Maybe the snowball fights were a clue. Dutch had some cousins, boy cousins, across the street, across the three-tiered plaza that was and still is the Concourse. Donnie, Lonnie, and Mikey, each in his own way a smart aleck bully hooligan. Each committed to maximum boy bravado and to their collective *force majeure*.

Colonies of like-minded children infested the place. Dutch was an outsider. It worked like this: you were chosen by a gang. Your gang patrolled the labyrinths of its territory, spied on each other, recruiting scouts while stockpiling snowballs, sticks and stones, missing no opportunity for gratuitous face-smashing, for gut-crunching, tear-making kid violence. We lacked cudgels, maces, boiling oil…bereft of weapons, ordnance, artillery, damage was nonetheless done. This was a school of hard knocks, a boys' academy of punches, kicks and wallops. Ever get body slammed into a solid marble wall? I did. And believe me, it was no picnic, I can assure you of that.

For a very short time—before his headlong plunge into occultism—Dutch had a love affair with the funny books. Dutch read them at lunch, pored over his superheroes as he put away mouthfuls of salami and mustard on white, stuffing it down, rapt in his tabloid devotions…mindlessly feeding himself chips of potato, his eyes roaming like unrequited lovers over the newsprint, the funny papers, the comics. One time a gang member tore a funny book from Dutch's hand and threw it—threw it, I say!—into a nearby puddle. Instantly the book was soaked through. Soaked through, as in, completely ruined. That was the first and last time I saw Dutch weep. Dutch, as I hope to explain, was thick-skinned, a veteran of inner pain; but this pain, this pain was outrageous... watching Green Lantern drown in rainwater like that, well, this was something else. This was genocide, an all-consuming loss. This was stars, comets, meteors, pulsatile waves of rage...this was violation. He put up his dukes. *I might be hurt*, he thought, *but let 'em at me, cause they can't do that to Dutch, let's see 'em try...*

Chapter 14

Victor's Grandpa Schmiel

Schmiel snarled and grimaced at the ultramondaine appointments of the room. Red velvet walls, black fish eggs on gilt-edged plates floating like bulls' eyes around the room. The supper club—not exactly a *Poe's Cozy Nook*—was hung like a veil from the jeweled brow of West 57th Street, thank you. I feel my discomfort accelerating, little shock waves, at first dull, then pounding, a burgeoning awareness of the abject stupidity of my choice.

The ghosts of Samarkand hovered in the room. Ghosts of Crimean Tartars spilled the guts of peasants—no free lunch there!—who, good soldiers all, disemboweled Jews.

It wasn't long before the snarling began.

Especially after a quick but hazardous reading of the italicized Francophile bill of fare.

I don't remember if we stayed.

For argument's sake let's suppose we did. For argument's sake I grabbed his nuts and in a psychic chokehold, insisted that he get with the program, that he order some fucking food.

Schmiel the man had reached his seventieth year; had lost his wife; had achieved a new girlfriend; had retired. There was a lot on his plate—just not caviar. Still, he was my grandfather and his cruel Lemurian stare had me transfixed. What a story! Decades of soul-numbing work had taken their toll. Broken his back. He didn't have much of a library at home but he let us frolic in the mangrove swamp of his tepid imagination. He kept the skeletal remains of a Victrola in one closet...the only closet...he kept discs, black vinyl music-bearing discs, each the thickness of a dollar, each the weight of a brick. Victor Herbert...There were porcelain trifles, Austro-Hungarian trinkets, mirrors propped on satin pillows...snarling but impotent photos of leering grandchildren...but he would not I say WOULD NOT speak of the Old World. The purpose of the restaurant, the caviar, the dinner was to get him to talk. (Yes, it was his birthday...we foundered at this, the barest pretext of celebration.) The man as was incapable of joy. Pleasure was something foreign, except perhaps in the subtlest and coarsest of his secret pre-Cossack dreams. Corset dreams, women with whalebone-hewn stays: that's what really turned him on.

How would I know? The cigars. The cigars that figured so prominently in his pictures. The black corsair sedan, maniacally polished, his main pride and joy. Belvedere? Buick? Dodge? Already I have strayed far from credibility: more lapses in memory are still to come. My grandmother rarely spoke. Bouts of enthusiasm, perhaps, great smells: it was in her lair that I learned the mysteries of 'cold cream.' A mist of balsam, a clinic for the working poor in Vienna, a vigorous nettle thrashing in Bessarabia, all this and more: first generation fragrances from so many years ago.

So: he was furious at me but he cosseted his rage—even when I stuck him with the bill. The price of love. After all, what are families for? The evening was a tender sacrifice for the issue of his loins, two generations removed. At another time, in another place, I would indicate my preferences, the ridiculous approximations of appetite of a ten year old boy. Items sprang off delicatessen menus like phoenixes, delectable free range chimeras. I was in a waking deli trance. Sour tomatoes. Brisket. Pastrami. Corned beef, extra lean…I ordered a beverage—Saratoga Geyser—and the waiter, his jagged forehead breached by moving veins (just like Schmiel's!), returned with a frickin' jeroboam of the stuff. My lot to quaff. Schmiel—grandpa—with his signature snarl: *Sit down before I knock you down…*! More than once I risked gastric tamponade rather than incur his wrath. I was scared to death so I finished my plate. Another time I force fed myself a bell jar's worth of pickles, the wretched vegetables, limpid and dill-choked, skipping from barrel to gullet like salmon dancing gaily upstream.

One time he bought a canary, freshly killed. Even as I child I would not consign Schmiel to the flames—flames he had seen first hand, flames he knew all too well. Behind his back, during stolen moments (he was busy throttling grandma Yetta), I would pry. When you are small, small as a child, it is easier to probe, easier to vanish behind maple nightstands and delve among the *objets trouvés*, delve among their things.

The bedroom was a Hungarian-Romish-Transylvanian paradise. I was confused. Why did he keep saying he was from Russia? I mentioned the porcelain…worked statuary, lacy and brittle, fantastic figurines airy and latticed as fine sea spray. 'China' they called it. There was nothing of whimsy, nothing of shoddy craftsmanship anywhere in that room. No paper calendars there! Only framed portraits, hints and glimmerings of another realm, another world, a ten year old's passport to adventure…Hapsburg? It was in that room that I inherited a healthy respect for Bismarck and the little I knew about all he had done.

I crept about, adhering I know not why to a self-imposed embargo on sound. Cabinet doors opened themselves as I traipsed from closet (I recall shoe trees clotted with cordovan) to moth balls to 'Kiwi Brand' shoe polish cans stacked like ordnance awaiting the cannon's maw.

Then I found it: the book. I held it in my hand, felt its weight, the moleskin smooth and taut against the slightly moist prominence of the ball of my palm.

And what was this? An inscription: *Varázslatos elójegyzési napló?*

LATER—much later—I learned this meant, Magickal appointment book or more freely translated, 'Occult Diary.'

Finally I understood: Schmiel was after big game. Everything he said, everything he did, was a fabric of lies.

Like a firebrand, the book singed my flesh.

Imagine what it did to him!

Was Grandpa the historical Franz Bardon, the famed Hungarian occultist tortured by the Nazis during the war? Was Grandpa practicing Kabbalah?

Chapter 15

25th Century Rand

He knew the riff about dying: no one gets out of here alive, etcetera. He took a class at the Academy of Sorrow where they paid you to tighten your nerves. Thickened your skin to the consistency of bone.

He learned a thing or two about himself. A couple of things about the species, too.

This was not the jungle. This was not about keeping fit. Well... maybe that was part of it, eating and sleeping properly, just to stay alive. Keeping the neural networks in shape.

The toughest part by far was the wrestling. Wrestling the thought-forms was the toughest part. They kept pace with you. The tougher you got, the more wily the thought-forms became. Spouting epithets in Hungarian was useless. His brothers at the college lit entire cities with the compost heat of their minds.

The Science of Mind. A warrior thing, Rand thought.

He practiced blindness. He found an old twisted piece of iron, evoked and crossed swords with phantom adversaries in the dusk.

The teacher zipped him up in the skin of a jaguar and threw him into a hall of mirrors.

Rand slew three Medusas in the dark. He danced the exercise

of hideous cacophony. Took the crooked baton and lead a troop of howling minions (Tennyson would have been proud.) Still he had to take nerve pills! A second exercise placed him martyr-like at the stake.

Then Rand was captain of the ship. Rand: a galactic navvy facing the challenge of his life: replace the ship's water closet with a septic tank—while hurtling through space at infra-light speed. In prison stripes Rand took on the task of jailing his heart.

He was strong, he was young, he was foolish. He could bring himself off in the dark. But to finish himself off without sound, without air…these were privations Rand could not bear.

One by one his chakras burned. He resigned himself to one or another form of retinal cancer but he got his break at last. The meridians flowed, oozed, toasting the margin between Rand and not-Rand. His physical envelope relaxed. Straightaway he mailed himself to Gautama; the vital energy, the *prajna paramita*, finally tamed and put to good use.

This perpetual student had lunch with Christ, popping the cork on countless demijohns as he toasted the grateful belching mob.

Rand slithered, an aberrant soul on a shoestring budget. Retinas and erectile tissue poised, a superhuman thermocouple straying into the red. Not just another cyborg: he was Rand, a juggernaut! (So what if his atomic fingerprint was lit up in krypton at every way station from Andromeda to Luna Park?)

Rand assumed dog form, then pointed. Juggernaut terrier, pointing but unable to weep! He almost made Varsity (first cut for the cryogenics squad: not bad, not bad at all.) But the rat-faced commodore kept farming him out to the colonies…where Rand underwent cardiac frag. He crawled back under his rock;

that didn't help either. His partner Solomon Hemingway insisted on presiding at his [own] auto-execution.

Second semester Rand was asked to invent and then destroy cosmology. He burned books, including an obscure tract crafted by Cioran (some gimcrack manifesto on neural networks, bearing the gimcrack title The Problem with Being Born.)

Rand fasted. Just when he was asked to face his Maker, juggernaut Rand fell asleep at the wheel. Face God? No thanks!

Rand's billion digital hookups held tight. He liked to watch drownings. Especially when sharks were involved. The predator/prey equation and all that. This kind of poem didn't come cheap. Rand swallowed five Bibles in one short night.

Chapter 16

Is Dutch Schultz Still Alive?

Where he came from no one really knew. Did he pop out, full grown, from the gravid pages of kabbalah? Arthur Flegenheimer—'Dutch'—was a snot-faced geek from (then) Jewish Harlem. (Or was it Brooklyn? The Bronx?) In the twenties he rode sidecar on Rothstein's whiskey truck. He didn't hang with the preppy crowd—unless you think guys like Bo Weinberg, Ticktock Tannenbaum, and Lulu Rosenkrantz were cardigan-sporting rowers. Dutch's cronies majored in 'humanities': namely, rackets, extortion, the numbers game. They busted heads outside Lindy's, nowhere near Harvard Square. Dutch was tough, a sharpie—trouble in any crowd. Trouble was his middle name. He had a big bent nose, an unforgiving mouth, dark Mediterranean eyes. One girl said he reminded her of Crosby—Bing Crosby, with his face hopelessly bashed in.

Things looked grim. The feds thought they had him. Income tax evasion. The grand jury convened in Malone, a fly speck on the map of upstate New York. Dutch moved headquarters to the town's only hotel. Moved lock, stock, and barrel to a small hotel; made nice to the porter; gave candy to the locals. He dressed down. 'Only queers wear silk shirts,' he was heard to say.

A week before the trial he went into a local church and converted. Arthur Flegenheimer reinventing himself, morphed into exemplary: a Catholic, a sure-shot contender for sainthood when the time was right.

The jury, asked to deliberate, was stymied, hung, minus a verdict. Schultz, now Malone's mayor, had bribed the entire town.

Lucky Luciano once boasted, 'The loudmouth is never coming.' Luciano was wrong.

'It's a tough world where there ain't no place for dunces,' Dutch told reporters. 'And the Dutchman ain't no dunce,' he said. 'And as far as I'm concerned, Alcatraz doesn't exist. I'll never see Alcatraz.'

Bo Weinberg, duly fitted with cement shoes, got himself wacked—dumped without ceremony in the East River.

Dutch and the boys continued meeting nightly at the Palace Chop House in Newark.

Chapter 17

The Kabbalah According to Dutch

WHETHER DUTCH SCHULTZ was born in Brooklyn or in the Bronx is immaterial. We know that Schultz was carrying on famously as a racketeer. Dutch's henchmen stopped at nothing to please their Führer.

Schultz never married though he did like to have a good time. During his self-imposed exile upsstate, Schultz acquired a working knowledge—*Stabat Mater*!—of alchemy and kabbalah. Needless to say (so why say it?) Schultz did not consider alchemy a way to 'self-knowledge.' It was a path of self-promotion. Finding the frickin' Philosopher's Stone might be the greatest—the only—good. But not for Dutch. The Stone! The apocryphal rock that held within its quartz and feldspar veins all the secrets of nature. According to Schultz's teacher, the sacred wisdom could be found in one book. One book only. So what if Dutch was illiterate? Right away he put his best men (Bo Weinberg, a prolific killer; Abbadabba Berman, best numbers runner around; Lulu Rosenkrantz, a freewheeling sharpshooter) on the case: soon enough every used bookshop on Fourth Avenue was cased, razed, reduced to cinders and ashes.

ONE NIGHT SCHULTZ dreamed an angel. Standing before him with outstretched hands, the angel said, 'Look Dutch, take a gander at this here parchment in my hands.' The light from the book was blinding. 'This here book will give you confusion, headache, *agita*...but one day you will find that which you seek—that which no other man has seen. Trust me.'

A man on death row handed the mysterious volume to Schultz. It was bound in dull metal, its pages replete with strange diagrams, with signs and sigils that Schultz could not for the waning life of him work out. The pages were thin, formed of pressed butterfly wings. The writing was not very clear. Aramaic? Or the scribblings of a demented yardbird, positing meanings where none could possibly exist? Schultz was able to make out the name of the author, someone who called himself Abraham the Jew. One thing was clear: anyone who tampered with the book would have a curse on his head to the end of all time.

Not a worrier by nature, Dutch nonetheless kept wondering about the book. Was it really for him? Was he qualified for an undertaking like this? The secrets of life and death lay between the covers of the mystic volume. On the other hand...Dutch already knew the secrets of life and death. How long ago had he lost count of those he had sent on to the next world? He needed a mentor, a rabbi, someone who would be willing and able to help him solve the riddle...the riddle of the book.

There are no coincidences. Enter Franz Hector Deutsche . From Dutch's Alcatraz journal:

I first met Dr. Franz (Franz Hector Deutsche to you) at an outdoor café. The opera was in town. Fragrance on the wind, birds aloft, singing to the sky.

I was not in a great mood. My mood was darker than usual.

Each bird the soul of a drowned child borne aloft, as the crow flies. Frankly, it was all a bit much. An allergic twinge, then I sneezed. I sneezed again—twelve times in all. I clutched at my napkin. Did I say napkin? There was none. It was a filthy handkerchief, monogrammed in the usual sporty way. The next aerosol volley floated on the skin of my cabernet. The man at the next table offered his handkerchief. 'Go ahead, take it. Twelve, by the way, is a lucky number.' I refused. He dismissed my gesture then without stopping he reeled off some long cockamamie story. Something about a medieval rabbi in Lubhlinwho like me had had to sneeze twelve times. 'Like you...' I balled the handkerchief up. I eyed it, the Doc, the street with dejection. 'You're lost, aren't you?' 'Not exactly lost,' I said. 'More like...searching.' He considered.His beret was the color of stale mustard. The hat made a permanent shadow over his roving eye. I had already sneezed. I had ruined my handkerchief, not his. Now the bum was ruining my day. I abandoned the wine. The snot would not sink. We watched it congeal. It turned me off. Coffee. Coffee would do me better. 'Listen, young man.' There was something about him. His movements gave an impression of power. A slight turn of the head, a flick of the finger...there was something snake-like about him. Something stronger than TNT... Handing me his business card, Deutsche looked past, beyond, through me. Meantime a pigeon picked at some crumbs. 'That bird will live forever,' he said. No sooner had he paid his bill than he was lost among the crowd. A con artist, I thought. Another nut, another screwball wandering loose in the city. Maybe the dachshund on the corner was Wendell Wilkie; maybe I would run carrier pigeons from a rooftop in Labrador...

But the professor was right.

His words had triple meanings.

The very next week an old wound flared.

Once again I was beside myself, wracked with miserable pain...

Face it, Dutch: your life is a mess! Problems at home, problems on the job, too much pressure. I was fit to blow my top.

Deutsche was right: I was lost! I found his business card beneath a dues notice from the lodge. It read:

Franz Hector Deutsche, M.D. Medical Kabbalah. Beneath the name was his address and phone.

NEXT THING you know, I get a package in the mail. Postcards sandwiched between the pages of a very strange book.

Okay...Deutsche worked exclusively in dreams.

He promised to fix me, promised to rid me of astral filth.

He would clean my inner house.

I am schooled, Deutsche wrote, in the method of Paracelsus. Do you know the name? You have heard of Fludd, of Nicholas Flamel? Regardless, I expect to be paid on time.

Catchy! I liked it. So I called him. Threatened him, too. We arranged to meet.

FOR TWENTY ONE sleepless nights Schultz pondered the meaning of the book. None of his cell mates, no one on heaven or earth— let alone in Alcatraz—could possibly help.

Later, thanks to a friend in Havana, he gathered the laboriously worked (translated from Hebrew to Sanskrit to Brooklynese) material for the alchemical transmutation. Dutch strictly followed the method of Abraham the Jew, first changing a silver dollar into a dime, then transforming rubbing alcohol into absinthe. The gangster's heart bloomed. The eternal spirit had at last emerged.

DUTCH struck it rich. In his hands, everything turned to gold. Thanks to the sacred book, Dutch had risen above the brute gratification of the senses. Immortality, he now knew, was obtained only at the highest price: the victory of spirit over matter. Dutch made sure that each of the men he gunned down over the next 11 years understood this too. For Dutch, death held no mystery. Purgatory had no charm; life held no puzzles. There was no problem that a bullet could not solve. Somehow it helped to know that when the time came, the dead would return in myriad forms to work on themselves, only to die anew.

ADEPTHOOD. There is but one test to determine spiritual superiority: that being an abiding lack of contempt for riches.

The Last Mile. Schultz never made it to the chair. If he had, he would have cracked jokes all the way. Instead, he was gunned down in a family restaurant in Hoboken.

These bon mots—Dutch's last words—were uttered between 4 and 6 pm on 24 October 1935. The gentleman was drunk on fever, fever from a pullulating gunshot wound deep in his gut.

At Fahrenheit 106, Dutch's rhapsody went like this:

"Now listen Phil, fun is fun. Aha...Please!
Papa! What happened to the 16?...Please
make it quick; fast and furious; please...

fast and furious…I'm getting my wind
back, thank God! You go ahead with the
dot and dash system. Whose number is
that in your pocketbook? Phil?…

'Oh, oh, dog biscuit, and when
he is happy he doesn't get snappy…
You didn't meet him; you didn't even
meet me; the glove will fit what I say.
Oh, Cocoa, no…thinks he is a
grandpa again and he is jumping
around. No, Hoboe and Poboe
think I mean the same thing."

TRANSLATED to Hebrew, then assigned their respective numerologic value, Shultz's last words reveal the secret of the Emerald Tablet of Hermes, the Philosopher's Stone, and the transmutation of metals.

Chapter 18

The Prison Psychiatrist

Rand was deeply troubled. Always had been. As a child, Rand wrote advertising copy instead of playing hooks and ladders. Then he transferred to the human services agency.

'You'll make some girl very happy someday!!!' his mother said. This and everything else he heard he reflexively spat out. Revulsion and disgust his constant companions. He tried but failed to negotiate the narrow path between dialectical materialism and true creature comfort.

The sun boosted then fractured his spirit. The sound of the human voice set his nerves on edge. Rand watched the world from above, as from an aerie. He chose broiled, not sautéed.

The writing group wasn't enough for Prisoner #181924. He hastened to the prison doctor, a strange and elusive man called Deutsche. Franz Hector Deutsche. Why Deutsche chose to spend his time in those rank corridors, rubbing elbows and trading secrets with the lowest of the low, was a mystery.

Rand retired his crayon (the only writing instrument permitted him) and let it rip. Dr. Deutsche wanted to know why. Why had Rand killed his wife?

"The atrocities documented in the proceedings at Nuremberg,

short of hanging and gassing, have been committed against me...
all in the name of marriage.

"The actual list will set your teeth chattering, doctor; the list is
long, interminable, intolerable..."

Deutsche gave as good as he got: he said nothing.

"...but includes defamation, moral defloration, derogation,
slander, libel, Aspergillus, verbal abuse, taunting, mockery, belittling, emasculation, character assassination, devaluation,
ball-busting, betrayal, desertion, negligence and cruelty."

Rand was getting worked up.

Gail liked to sic—a monomanical pitbulll—she liked to sic
[sic] the police on Rand. Her anthology of trumped up charges
was longer than a nineteenth-century catalogue of Sears: He had
threatened her, he was violent, a drunk; not only that, but Rand
was insane, he had threatened to dump her in the river. She came
home late from liaisons, from dinners with secret boyfriends,
boyfriends all named Marilyn if you believed her and her ersatz
confessions.

What a glorious day, when the stalwart of the community, the
avatar of decency, was stopped by the police: pronto, he would
have to vacate his home.

Gail treated him as though he simply was not there. She put
on a long chiffon gown, pretending in her whimsy to escort him
to the agency ball. Instead, she had him stop the car: Rand could
walk the remaining distance to Bridgeport alone. She wasn't
going. Gail's imperious stance left Rand half-cocked, fumbling
with his balled up tuxedo, cummerbund, and suspenders on the
service ramp of the interstate. The jet stream from a passing
18-wheeler whipped the tip of his rented bowtie right into his

eye. It hurt something awful but he managed to wrest the item back into place.

Gail Rachel was in her glory. If Gail was frightened by a bee; if a screen door needed tightening; if the trash needed taking out: she knew what to do. She called Kevin or Peter or Michael—any of the men on the lane. Any man on the lane could handle domestic situations better than Rand. They comprised Gail's bullpen, cockswains in waiting for her irresistible call. Everybody knew.

Gail flipped. She went into high Torquemada mode.

"Say more, Vic," said Dr. Deutsche.

"I should have seen it coming, doc. this particular descent into hell…twelve years in the making, sliding faster and faster down the black hole to nowhere. It was foreshadowed, reverse Kismet minus the belly dancers, minus the girl.

"It wasn't long before she went out nights. One time I met her at a bar. Diana the Huntress, with her pious audience in tow: boys, girls, ponies, parents, uncles, aunts, cousins…

But her eyes! Her eyes were brown, eyes as big as the moon. No getting away from them. Gail's eyes…I got sucked right in. Stand up, step up to the line, play out the comedy of sexual manners, play it to the hilt. Imagine: I stood in line, got her number and a promise to meet.

"I was lonely, stupid, ripe for affection. Ripe for the picking: a fool for her love.

"My only comfort this meandering horseshit of a convo with you…"

Chapter 19

Taking Out the Wife

Was his soul wracked by violent antipathies—or was Gail Rachel just another reptile, equally abhorrent to any vertebrate she might meet?

Rand was a rat, a rodent digging its burrow, lining it with the pathetic tailings and *objets trouvés* of the disinterested 'natural' world (including, he flattered himself, the flotsam and jetsam skidding off the remaindered canvases of Hieronymus Bosch…)

All of the crimes that one person can foist on another, every form of violence known to man and beast, had been committed in the name of marriage, on Rand.

His doctor, Hector Felix Deutsch, began to weep. Not from the pain but from the unremitting boredom of it all.

"Want the laundry list?"

"Why ask? You're going to tell me anyway, no?"

"Defamation, deforestation, moral defloration, derogation, rupture of limbic hymen (trust me: men have these too), slander, libel, verbal abuse, taunting, mockery, betrayal, emasculation, neovascularization, strangulation, vagina dentata, character assassination, devaluation, global recession, ball-churning, besmirching, poor diction, bad taste, negligence and let's not forget cruelty. Stepping with muddied feet on my precious plus-fours.

"This harridan, this monstrous eruption vomited from her mother's cursed cloaca—that doomed stoma should have been sewn shut long ago, sealed over a thousand times—this hideous belch from the volvulus of Satan...her feculent ranting robbing me of what little remained of myself...How is it, I ask you, that such a person walks the earth, sleeps at night, breathes God's good air?

"'I married my worst nightmare. I married a cunt."

"Sweet. Is there more?"

"It all depends, doc. How much time do we have?"

Chapter 20

Your Marriage Sound Like This?

She throws you out. Out of house, out of home, out of her heart.

Living in the car, yogurt containers and last year's dirty socks sprouting penicillin beneath the seat.

Dog! You've enjoyed every motel on that miracle mile. Watched every pay-to-view movie, stroked yourself to oblivion, Zohar in hand. You're getting stronger every day. No one tells you what to do! Wear what you want, dude; shower when you want. Play air guitar till dawn.

"Call her Wonder Woman, doc. She keeps me focused. That's why I freaked…after what I did. Can't imagine a world without her…How about you, doc? Cat got your tongue?"

Hector Franz had long since passed out.

Chapter 21

Take Out Menu

exploding tennis ball

exploding tampon

anaphylactic bee in Dixie cup

assassin

lesbian frotteuse (poison)

Suicide Manor

kabbalah

pink roses

death as spiritual homework – something she 'needs' to do

scorpion in sneaker

ten seconds in my world

gut shot (bow and arrow)

gut shot (cross bow and arrow)

Gillette frags in egg salad

cannibalism

power surge

pillow

Voudon

Chapter 22

Deutsche's Second Chance

"Wake up man!"

How dare Deutsche talk to him like this?

Rand adjusted the visor on his cap. Don't react.

"Pardon?"

"Demonocacomania."

"Say what?'

"Demonocacomania."

"You lost me, pal."

"As in, lycanthrocacomania."

"Oh: sex with werewolves."

"Creatures who feed on the spiritual essence of others."

"Astral larvae!"

Suddenly Deutsche felt sick. This guy would never get better. Even worse, he would never shut up.

Rand droned on.

"...the unappreciated rolê of succubi and incubi in the deterioration of modern life."

"Talk Victor, let it all hang out... Lose that dybbuk!"

So he did. 'Pillow. From the hotel. Stripes, soiled; oiled by many heads. Watching the legs flail.

"Erotic frenzy. Me and Gail on a date."

"Victor, these are psychic remnants. Your spirit has been cannibalized whole."

Chapter 23

Lulu

Lulu Rosencrantz, one of Dutch's pals, 'sat' for Old Sparky (an overused and greatly maligned euphemism for the electric chair.)

The following turned up in Lulu's charred pockets.

Lulu wrote:

"For Dutch sexual union was an animal act.
He enjoyed it but at the same time he couldn't
get away fast enough. Sex for Dutch was an
immediate reminder of his excreta-tainted
racial memory. He wished to be annihilated
during the act of love: longed for spontaneous extinction
in the thrall of sexual embrace. So what if it took
a bullet? He often wondered: were these desires sick,
against nature? Did normal guys have them too?.
Was he to be counted among the sexually
insane? Or were his urges mere prevarication,
poorly veiled semantic thrusts?
  "I watched the man. He would have laughed
all the way to the chair (had he gone that route.)
I imagine a shudder, long suppressed, coursing through him,

sending a collective *Gasp!* through the crowd.
They have no idea…Who dreamed that Dutch
had such spirit, such wind? Divine afflatus…A mist, a
great miasmia, more beautiful than light."

Chapter 24

The Kabbalah According to Dutch

Dutch Schultz took a correspondence course. By taking copious notes he killed motes of time. Kabbalah lessons by mail. The doctor, Deutsche, feigned mild interest. The Kabbalah school sent sham affection (better than the real thing, for Dutch.) What the fuck! Any way you looked at it he was going to fry. Might as well live it up, enjoy, enjoy!

Dutch put on a new face during the last weeks of his life. Arthur Flegenheimer became the remote teacher's pet. A model student. He stayed up nights, smoking, hawking up phlegm—and writing too.

(He tried to hand the papers to the bailiff. Dutch never raised his voice—a perfect gentleman to the very end. Who knew that Dutch's lock-down writing would ever be tattooed on the arms of millions across the sea?)

Several passages survive his ordeal:

Lalah Qabbalah by Dutch Schultz, Sing-Sing

The pit yawned at his feet—poor tired Pit. The sky
loomed a unicorn tapestry (maybe it was a satin brassiere
trailing among the clouds.) Something was singing. Some

maniac down the corridor—singing. Séance or stool
pigeon? Open sesame, motherfucker!

It was 1935 and the kind man loved science.
The criminal mind dissolved in the suds of science.
This time it was Death Row…but his imagination
never let him down. It was the squirrels…
[illegible]…He never went hungry, he never walked
alone. The happy mobster glowed. Heraldry,
ley lines ablaze from Avebury to Flatbush. Velvet
drapery thrown aside: make way for the Creatures
of the World! Winged Victory of Samothrace! So what
 if he roasted in the chair? Do what thou wilt shall be
the whole of the Law…
'Only the strong survive.' The Lion.
Heraldic lion?
After the animals the Planets arrive. They
want nice beach property…they don't ask for much.
Garden apartments in Jersey. Even Henry Plantagenet
bought one: a garden apartment in New Jersey, that is.
Planatagenet went for the triple bypass. Old men ate borscht;
they got blow jobs too. *Ess, ess mein Kind*…These had to
filthiest words on the planet. Pellets, Planets, Plantagenets:
surreal prostheses in the service of love. Better to
go down in glory, better the bullet than the cracked
porcelain vase of confusion.
Field mice, water rats, scampering up the
walls of the pit. More prey, better love…

This note, a citation from Alfred Lord Tennyson, was found crammed between the sole and leather of Dutch's boot: "I never had any revelations through anaesthetics, but a kind of waking trance—which I have frequently had, quite up from boyhood, when I have been all alone. This has come upon me through repeating my own name to myself self silently, till all at once, as it were out of the intensity of consciousness of individuality, individuality itself seemed to dissolve and fade away..."

Small comfort for a man about to fry.

Dutch dreamed a colony of anorectic handmaidens.

Between February 9 and March 12 he resided (in his mind) in the Olsen home in Ballerup, a suburb of Copenhagen.

And:

Gail Rachel, you have no idea. How much I
love you. How much I love you...I am a
bleeding angel in your hands. Bleed me.
Use me. Twist me like putty. Knead me,
knife me, spread me like grout.
You have robbed me of sleep forever.
That's the least of it.You
have cracked the vessel of my sanity. In
the guise of a handmaiden Gail you turned
me out of the house. Sure I made you cry.

Sure I did you wrong. Sure your sister
Ceil turned my head. I'm not made out
of stone. You left your calling card on my
brain.
Sheer autobiography—a fucking
mirror. That's the problem. I denied you.
 I put you down. I peed in the
stream of your waking consciousness.
I took the hymnal of your innards and
turned them into a stinking heap.
 I am confirmed in these beliefs by
a careful reading of Schopenhauer.
Arthur, I hear you say, calm the fuck down.
Arthur can't and neither can I.
Schopenhauer didn't stick around long enough.
He's waiting for me, there in the other place.
I am going to meet him there. I am green lint
hiding beneath the cicada's wing A stinking
piece of lint, I tell you, sublime detritus
that will never make it to hallowed ground.
To will is to sin. The contemplation
of truth and beauty a bagatelle.
A luxury, Gail, that we cannot afford.
Had enough? Will you take these
jejune ravings to heart, as you sit
calmly behind the plate glass. hands
in lap, watching me fry? Glad to be rid of me at last? I bet.
My sweet love. We will be together,
forever, I can promise you that.

You and me and your sister Ceil. It's wrong.
I know it's wrong. But how can love ever
be wrong?
Tell them to wrap your undies around
my face when they throw the switch.
Do I want music? Whatever
works for you. Believe me doll: I never
wanted it to end this way.
The shadow of Baudelaire
haunts my soul. That son of a bitch!
Fucking Baudelaire hung me out to dry.
I asked for baked Alaska; I got verdigris instead.
   How's dad? They say you ejaculate at the moment
of truth. Put that sexy hand where it belongs—
right between your legs. Save some love juice for
me. I don't care about Ceil, only you.
The chaplain says he'll give me a
cigar.
The Ideal is living, vital, real! What
kind of caviar do we want, my Gail?
My sidereal dreams will leave you breathless,
haunted and vacant like an abandoned lot in
the Bronx. Rimbaud? Throw him a bone. Let his
dog breath be. I'll hunt him down, and believe me—
I'll find him.
Split the infinitive, babe. The Sphinx
holds the reins, the Leopard rides sidecar…
In another life I was a starveling, an abandoned
child king.

Trust me: I'll be around.

Someone's sick idea of a joke:
Associated Press. Ossining, NY:
Arthur 'Dutch' Flegenheimer walked the Last Mile today. He
declined the customary last meal, insisting that onlookers endure
his favorite poem (Rimbaud):

Off I would go, with fists into torn pockets pressed
My overcoat became a wrap of mystery
Under the great sky, Muse, I was your devotee.
Ah, what fine dreams I had, each one an amorous guest.

My only trousers gaped behind; and thus I went
Tom Thumb the dreamer, husking out some lyric line
My nightly inn had always the Great Bear for its sign
My stars moved with a silken rustle of content.

And often, sitting by the roadside, I would listen,
On calm September evenings, with fine dew a-glisten
Upon my brow, like drops of cordial, sweet yet tart,

Where, rhyming in these shadowy, fantastic places,
As if I played a lyre, I'd gently pluck the laces
Of my burst boots, one foot hugged tight against my heart.

Gail (he wrote) you fill me. My heart is bursting at the thought
of you.

One of Dutch's 'cahiers' bore the following quote (you guessed it: Schopenhauer) on the flyleaf:

"…People of a strange and curious temperament
can be happy only under strange circumstances,
such as suit their nature, in the same way as
ordinary circumstances suit the ordinary man;
and such circumstances can arise only if, in some
extraordinary way, they happen to meet with
strange people of a character different, indeed,
but still exactly suited to their own. That is
why men of rare qualities are seldom happy."

I'LL DRINK to that. Dutch quaffed the flagon. Dutch spanked the monkey. He played with himself several thousand times before they shackled his hands and taped his lunatic grin shut.

A woman who came to visit was paid to kiss him on the mouth.

No one got to see his reading matter. Lives of the Saints. In the prison library he studied Pater, Ignatius Loyola, ascetic practice.

DUTCH quickly tired of his cell mate Felix Deutsch. (No relation to the prison doctor with the same ill-starred name.) Felix took nicely to the tire iron, wielded in a loving, pensive manner by Dutch.

'My marriage is a failure. A complete failure.'

'You have failed as a man,' Dutch agreed. 'How about a bedtime story? A nice embedded story?'

Felix stared at him through the Venetian blind of his puffy blackened eye.

'Do I have a choice?'

Chapter 25

Rand in the Suburbs

Victor Rand enjoyed his home but this time he went too far.

His thoughts constantly wandered. Always the same dream—Helen of Troy on the divan, delivering him from the burden of choice, snatching him to safety from the freezer aisle in the supermarket, from the three ring circus of procreation, jealousy, and violence.

Rand had too much art. 'Art.' Sculptures and installations, hideous gew-gaws that provoked silence, triggered bouts of hysteria and swooning among his much put upon guests.

Not that he had many guests! It wasn't the art that kept them away. It wasn't the statue—a copy of the *The Winged Victory*, much larger than the original. So what kept them away? Plain and simple: whelking. Victor kept a whelk farm in the basement. It started out small, right behind the stairs. The ice cube trays couldn't contain them; nothing did. The nasty little things took over the stairs, the boiler and mud rooms, the entire house.

Victor had hobbies. He studied invisibility. Another time he studied hypnosis. A dreamer! He fancied Catherine de Medici, languid in his arms. Lucretia Borgia. Lois Lane. And why not?

A girl came over. Maybe this was it. He thought he impressed her but then he realized how deeply he had turned her off. Drink in hand, she was already imaging the next blind date.

"Anyone ever tell you you're a ringer for Britney?"

She rolled her eyes. 'Britney? Britney who?' Victor felt rejected, ruined, in deep despair.

Careful, Victor, he thought. You are a certified student, a diplomate no less, of anger management.

The girl was squirming, dying to get away. No matter. He explained how the famous psychiatrist Jung had cracked up, gone into hiding at Burghoelzli for over a year. No one cared. Still, Jung emerged a better man from his tango with madness. He brought gifts back from the depths: visions of a world wracked and riven, a world of leaf blowers, of white trucks and ice cream vendors, of light opera and risotto, and—talk about post cards from the edge—a world of nihilistic [blind] dates.

The girl was not impressed.

"Show me, don't tell me," she said.

Did she have a name? Did they make love? Did they have anything in common, other than an interest in Grace Metalious and the next world war?

Victor's background in science was impressive. The experiments in the basement spun out of control.

A torrent of poorly formed creatures, their little skeletons fused beyond recognition, crawled out on to the lane. The town was not ready for this. The police couldn't help.

The girl never came back.

Victor, beside himself with grief, considered dousing himself with the same life-denying potion that had spawned the mutants—but who wanted to spend his life as a biological sport?

The girl—he couldn't remember her name (Eudora? Chyna? Helen Powell?)—where was the girl?

His place was a mausoleum. Therefore I should decorate it like one.

Another girl, also called Gail, visited once. She kept asking if he had any DVDs. This Gail never heard of 'Samothrace.' She wanted to know how many cars Victor owned.

Rand lived for visits from girls like Gail. Girls like Gail wanted nothing to do with him. Rand preferred monsters, miscreants, and misshapen sculpture to Merlot and Maseratis.

Then too, his sexual appetite was thin. If a girl stayed over, what would he do with her? Rand was a creature of habit. He could pursue any mania—except sex—with relentless and terrible vigor.

Rand envisioned crypts, vaulted and stony chambers that dragged the eye kicking and screaming to the world beyond.

Rand tarried among the pages of art history. He captained a wholly imagined team: Mirandola, Fludd & Flamel, Giordano Bruno…and the obscure bishop who with astral larvae desecrated the cathedral of St. Sulpice.

The last thing Rand wanted to do was disappear.

Rand took to bed. No word from Gail. He had dared to soar. He had dared to invite her, her and all the others, over. Hubris! Now he must fall.

Rand built a tomb.

It would play out like this: Rand would let the light of eternity blaze. Without Gail by his side he could have a nice cold bier. Rand could abandon himself to the nearest sepulcher at hand.

An early grave was too good for him. His final moments in the world would be drawn out. Rand could linger on the shore, starved for time (not to mention air) before crossed the mortal bar. He felt a twinge: regret. The little creatures, the ferrets-turned-felines (absent a limb or two) would miss him, terribly.

Something in Rand heaved. Snapped. How could he give up, just like that?

'I'll reach out,' he swore. 'I'll choose life,' he muttered, awash in grief.

Gail Pomerantz unlisted her number.

With gusto Rand embraced the task of entombing himself.

Filing away at the grout and mortar became his nightly routine. He looked forward to it. Come sundown, Victor was out there, a regular, avoiding the suspicious glances of the watchman, the landscaper. With chisel and fish knife, Rand pecked away at *Winged Victory*'s implacable façade. Yes, he would have preferred TNT. But the statue was far too delicate for that.

He looked forward to the strokes of the nail file, the adze. With bleeding fingertips Victor prised the mortar loose.

He worked it for months. He swept each night's filings into a velvet satchel. Rand's obsession flared the more he sacrificed sleep.

Precious sleep…soon he would sleep enough! Beneath the restive gaze of the uncaring world Victor would lie forever in his catafalque of plaster and cement.

Victor's parents had been admitted on separate occasions to Potter's field. He did not wish to join posterity in those meadows. He had not located the parental graves. Victor was a solitary. He despised protean solutions—not only to the riddle of life but to the riddle of burial as well.

Night after night he worked at *Winged Victory*.

At first the cavity was no bigger than a shoebox, a toaster oven. He placed a live pigeon in the space, then sealed it shut. He could just make out the flapping of the wing. The bird could not get free. The experiment was a success.

Rand exhumed the tiny body before it could stink.

Rand was intent on burying himself alive.

IN THE END he crawls into *Winged Victory*. Drinks several bottles of pills, washing them down with vegetable juice.

Seals himself in.

CHAPTER 26

RAND AND SCHULTZ

"Help man, I'm drowning."

"Your marriage. Say more."

"You sure?"

"No, I'm not sure."

"Where should I start?"

"Take it from the top, maestro."

"…We were in double decline. Tailspin."

"Track the dwindling star that is now your friggin' life."

"Gail…She had so many friends. That's why I started looking at her sister. Ceil."

"I know, I know. A real beauty."

"She had so many friends."

"So many attachments, infatuations, idolatries."

"Idealizations."

"You might say."

"I should have known from the start."

"From the get-go."

"She crushed my ego. Like a flea beneath a hammer."

"Satanic. You had less than a snowball's chance in hell. Plus she had her eye on that other guy."

"What other guy?"

"Murray. Murray Rand. A chiropractor, from Germany. Locked the door in his office, nailed her on the exam table. Hell, pal, you told me yourself."

Rand shed a tear.

"Leakage," Rand explained. "Sorry."

"Can the apologies. Go on." Dutch whipped the car antenna in a threatening manner. The metal sliced through the air but that was all.

"I was caught up in my own stuff."

"Issues. You had issues. Everyone has issues. It's called being human."

A gravid pause.

"You wanted to be heard." Dutch winked at his roommate.

"Adored."

"She took a dump on your Walter Benjamin. Broke the spine of your Spinoza."

"Tarnished my higher self."

"With a bitch like that on your back how could you be true to your self?"

Rand sighed. How he wished Gail was there. How he wished Gail was the one strapped to the gurney.

"The exigencies of time, of fate."

Dutch thought about his father. His father, shoving kippered herring down his bottomless hatch.

"Shut your trap," he said to no one in particular. "There's nothing worse than a stool pigeon."

"Except a dung beetle."

Rand went on. "I worked in a hospital, on the back ward."

"Electrocution ward?"

"Nah…Elocution ward."

"Where you met Ceil?" Dutch grimaced. What an imbecile. Imbeceil…

"That was Berenice, birdbrain. A photographer." Rand had had dirty thoughts: nailing Berenice in the men's room at the Met. Sloppy seconds for Vermeer.

"Stop pouting," Dutch said. "Enough with the tantrums."

"Like you said: I have issues."

They brought in a doctor. A quack.

"First things first," the charlatan explained. "Talk to me. Tell me about the loneliness in your heart."

"A vainglorious aerie," Rand tried to explain. The artist in his soul rebelled at the suggestion of nostalgia. To hell with that.

"I am in exile."

"You talk funny."

"I am divorced from the wellspring of beauty, forever at odds with my heart. Exiled from the oasis of my dreams."

Rand saw palm trees from the window. Nice, but crawling with bugs. That's why they're called palmettos.

The torpor of it all!

From the window the banana trees listed in a tentative breeze. A storm was brewing. More shit blowing in from the tropics.

CHAPTER 27

SCHULTZ AND RAND

SHE NEVER COMMITTED (to the marriage.) She was always on the phone. You could walk into the house with a gunshot wound, bleeding from the eyes, ears, and throat, and she'd motion, Give me a second—I'm on the phone.

Fuck that.

Her family was small. Tedious. Attachments like that were a dime a dozen. Point is, she wasn't there.

Her father?

Rand knew a thing or two about Pomerantz.

RAND barely survived his first ten years with the old man. Rand took up smoking to escape Pomerantz' suffocating invective. Pomerantz' war stories were like strychnine, attacking the nerves, shocking the sensibility into dissociated rhythms that clashed, frazzled, burnt themselves out. Mr. P., a classic textbook windbag, never gave his auditor a break. Being on the business end of that larynx was no laughing matter.

Amazing, how much one caught in the net of the first blush of romance was willing to forgive. How much you were willing to overlook. From where he was coming, of course, anything looked good. Already had thrown away half a lifetime by following his appetites. Was he a man...or was he a terrier?

Mr. P. was old. He fixed you with a grin that stopped just short of maniacal. He had stories about everything. A firing squad of sibilants and fricatives. A toxic rain of sputter. A horrid dew of I *told you so*'s. A nonstop circus of commentary, going the distance from cradle to grave. How many of his captive audience had already succumbed, suicided, fought their way across the threshold from this world into the next, to spare themselves one more moment of talk?

The first seven times Rand endured the man's diatribe he chalked it off: it was the price he had to pay, the vapid maunderings of a father about to hand off his daughter. The soporific fragrance of decaying meat...It was an exercise in self-discipline, in stone cold self-control. Then again, how far was he willing to go? Did Rand really want this girl?

Chapter 28

Dutch Kipling

From the desk of D. S.

I am sending along the following for publication in your gazette.

My father discovered these papers in an abandoned building on the city's upper west side. My dad, a purveyor of quality seafood, was a fishmonger, selling his wares from a stinking closet-sized shop. Forty years: if it swims we kill it! The shop was festooned with trinkets and collectibles plundered by his perspicacious hand from the recently deserted apartments of the recently deceased. Dad had an 'arrangement' with the cash-hungry superintendants, bellmen, and porters who minded the monolithic enclaves. These buildings were luxury liners, they stood Gotham proud, Dad's store was a whacked out mélange of paintings, *objets trouvés,* and prime fish filets. These so-called 'collectibles' were absolutely without value. Naturally, he gave them to me! I kept them, a haphazard collection of torpor-inspiring tokens from the ambiguous emotionally remote days of my garbage-plundering dad.

What can be said about this strange sheaf, this veritable feuilleton of Flegenheimania? I never knew the real Arthur Flegenheim. Or was it Flegenheimer—the real Dutch Schultz? The reader will find the document, though brief, to be erratic in the extreme. The extant manuscript skips at random from one cultural milieu (gangland) to another (Stanley and Livingston's Africa)—all in the blink of an eye. The narrative flits across history as though Dutch Schultz, this scion of the Pug Uglies, had been truly ominiscient, truly omnipresent across all cultures and epochs.

The unanswered questions are legion. I submit this curious document to the scrutiny of time; to the lasting judgment of history; and to the critical and patient eye of the reader.

Excerpts from Beyond Africa and Other Continents, by Arthur Flegenheim:

JASPER MUNGO. Reliable. Handlebar mustaches drooping. A man of the Book. Mungo was civilized, polished, a real Old Boy. Mungo's grandfather was an avid adherent to our cause in the Boer campaign. A dedicated parliamentarian, too.

Not much known about his father. His mother Constance had passed on too early for anyone's good. Plague? Jaundice? An aggravated case of dropsy?

Secret societies…Later I spent many hours pacing the floor, chain smoking, brooding over this. Jasper never mentioned such things—too personal. I suspected a disarming reticence on his part. Something was going on behind the imperturbable façade of the intercontinental engineer.

BERTRAN RUDEL. A svelte Belgian (an oxymoron, this?); Bertran was physician to our small party. Steeped in the arcana of tropical medicine, he specialized in the diagnosis (there was no treatment) of ophthalmoplegic crises induced by snakebite.

Very much a loner, Rudel kept to himself. Kept a journal, quite apart from the official record. I never looked at his scribbling. His hand moved across the page as though in a somnambulist's dream. His hand was a tiger, but he kept a pussycat in his heart.

Didn't sleep, never changed his clothes. What for? He actually did work up a sweat on occasion, but he never gave off that characteristic fetor, chemical wedding of sweat and sun, that varnishes the carapace of every perspiring, straining *homme d'Afrique*.

Rudel was first in his country's academy to veto governmental support of danger. Rudel was an incessant cartographer but since he never slept one concludes he never dreamed.

Enrique. our loyal, kind, brave slave. He was black as a bat out of hell.

The tender of camp fires; baker of breads; maker of meals. You never had to talk to the fellow. Your wish was his command.

On windless nights he lulled us to sleep with unintelligible songs of his far distant land. Plying his lutes and zithers, clapping miniature toe-drums, Enrique seemed an envoy from another world, a world at once unique and oblique to our own.

He portered, he schlepped, did yeoman's service across miles of hostile terrain. Ignorant of astrolabe, clueless with sextant, Enrique faultlessly steered us across desert and plain without complaint.

Top choice!

Caryn Felice. What a woman! What an explorer! Alexandra David-Neel had nothing on her.

At age three she asked for (and was promptly handed) an astrolabe. Compassed the phenomenological world from the purview of her playpen. Quadrilingual by age six. One year later she did her maths, creating insanely precocious gematria, her very own numerological schemes. She told her mama and her papa about her dreams; about how she would cross oceans, would meet the folk of all the nations whose strange tongues she had mastered so early on.

Caryn was nursemaid; companion; scientist; archetypal Woman to all.

A champion of bezique, a comfort during hard times—Dutch comfort minus the booze. She glowed with a lustrous interior beauty. And her rack was something to behold...Dressed in white, resplendent, back-lit by the dawning sun, she was for me an emblem of hope and fear. 'Anything is possible in this watery realm,' she said.

I did not know her age.

THE SMALL TERRAPLANE, now minus an engine, banked, shook and finally lowered itself into a life-saving bed of Sweet William. The vehicle took no damage but its occupants, abhorring the inexorable crash, feared soiling themselves.

Abandoned. The wavering plain; the strange brisk animals peering from the bush; the ferocity of the late midday early eventide sun—all these worked their nerves like a cyclone, a dervish of endless isolation, a mind-fuck of man pitted against nature and the certainty of death.

RUDYARD HEREFORD, the journalist of the group, also served as occasional 'navigator.' Numerous assurances of 'quite all right, thank you' were passed like party favors, like fava bean-inspired gas, but Hereford's assurances were nonsense—pure stuff and nonsense—reflexive reactive condolence, limpid and ineffective in the extreme.

Where were we? Hereford's map, sodden with his fellow passengers' vomit, lay broken, its meager hatchmarks and compass points fatally dripping from paper to blemish his starched and trembling knee.

Plane down, you say? Then spirits up!

A HYPOTHETICAL CAMERA angling in on the scene moments later reveals a sullen set of dreamers drowning in bogus poise.

There was the woman, Caryn, busy now with a peremptory inventory of the group's scattered effects. Clad in khaki, a yellow kerchief of Madagascar holding her silken tresses loosely in place, she would have stood Kipling proud. The triumph of civilization over the realm of shadow.

The Negro meantime waltzed effortlessly with the plane's unhinged door. At last he achieved an opening of sorts. His arms, bared to the shoulder, glistened like manioc in the dying light. He lowered crates by guy-wire down to the jungle floor. Enrique whistled, whistled remote tunes that soared and dove through impossible scales, inebriate quarter-tone oraisons through the spaces between his teeth. A bastion of brute endurance and courage. His devotion bordered on love…but why?

Rudel (the physician) quarreled with Mungo. Neither knew but each averred a best course of action. Rudel wanted to stay put, to pitch camp right there, take shelter beneath the plane's shattered wing. We could send out radio distress calls right then and there. Mungo wagged his head in rabid disbelief; I thought his agitated brainpan would slither out from his ear. His plan was different. He championed a quest for the interior. Uncharted territory, penetration of heartland—that kind of thing.

Evening. Better to shrug off the accumulating heat and our collective distress. Better to make camp for the night. Supplies intact, heads clear, compass needles a-pointing. A night beneath the open sky, then a day of work: hauling portage, defeating the myriad traps set by nature to keep us on this blasted continent for the ever-dwindling remainder of our days…

One week later. One of our party gone.

Five hours after crossing the equator, the terraplane developed engine trouble. The engine spat out clouds of dark smoke—as though disgusted with us and our unnecessary mission—bellowed dark smoke like great puffballs presaging our doom.

We landed—crash-landed, that is. A botanist's delirium…the plane bounced several times before accepting its final cockeyed berth among a magnificent stand of palm. We camped; we decamped. We worked hard to avoid making decisions. We argued over the food, over sleeping arrangements. Enrique watched the fracas with stoic indifference.

Darkness approached. Each hoped to see the morn. Slept well despite the continuous train of shadows that bent and swayed, mysteriously merged with thicket the evening through.

We were seasoned travelers, Dr. Rudel having been to Phuket twice.

The ceaseless croaking of the bullfrog has been known to drive men mad. The cry of jackanapes, the lugubrious howl of the jackal: all these pierced our night, transfixed our souls, like so many siren calls from hell.

What kind of place was this? Were we in Hell?

OUR SPIRITS rose with the coming of dawn. Miss Felice regaled us with plates of jam and bread. (We had not yet had our introduction to the native fare; this came later.)

We had set down on an island.

EQUIPMENT of portage, acquired at no little expense from Mssrs. Goodwin and Pribilof of Battersea, were set on braced backs. With a mighty heave-ho! I began hacking my way through dense cables of vine, hemp, mandragora. Even the fronds resisted our progress, giving back a hugely noisome belch of allergens, of pollen, at each transverse cut to the spavined leafs.

A large clear expanse loomed into view, Beyond this we made out a series of hills, hills and hummocks that undulated—even ululated! I thought—gently at the horizon's rim.

The wind was soft, carrying on its heels a trace of coolness that suggested more northern, more familiar climes. Countless tracts of mimosa...as Helios drove his chariot to the top of the sky you could make out—it was no mirage!—a river.

We saw a river.

Credit must be given where it is due. Mungo recognized the stream as an obscure tributary of the Gambia. Follow the present rivulet long enough and you find yourself contemplating the great stream of the central continent, the Niger. All hope of salvation, of not falling prey to this green hell, lay in finding the mother stream. Rudel scratched at his dandruff chin, perseverating at this.

He could not be talked down from fear. He was convinced that we had hit on uncharted territory. By Rudel's reckoning, we were lost.

THE NATURAL BIOLOGY of the Gambia is fascinating. But we were in no position to marvel at—let alone enjoy—the teeming life about us. Sharks, according to Losselard's Travels, are found in great numbers at the river's entrance from the sea. The hippopotamus shoal in large number as well. Miss Felice dubbed the sad creatures 'river-elephants'; she would have touched one were it not for the triumph of common sense over love.

THE HIPPO, who is amphibious, did not trammel our march to the sun. He feeds on grasses and such shrubs as the river bank affords. At the scent of man he is instantly gone. Or gores the unwitting observer to a bloody finish. Rudel could not be torn from his journal; he was in a dither, caught up in a self-imposed storm of scribbling and beard-pulling. I thanked my lucky stars: I was not from Belgium. Had the man invented his own science?

MOST STRANGE…even the Negro was daunted! By the most approximate calculation (we were not capable of more), we should have found some outpost, some tribal leavings, some little remnant of humanity.

We believe we are tracking the Gambia. We believe…Our dismay grows, palpable yet unvoiced. Enrique does as he is told. He offers no opinion—remains terse, mute to the point of madness—as to direction, goal, milestone.

We make camp. The parrots and mynahs are legion; anecdote has them snatching nursing babes from their mothers' arms. We shuffle wearily in place, plodding in sorry circles round the lonely campfire. Salt pork, canned curry, and a wary—we saw it!—tear dripping from Jasper's tired third eye.

"WE HAVE TO TALK." Thus I greet my companions the very next day. They stare, fixing me with the telescopes of their vacant eyes, their incomprehension muddied with imbecility, with disbelief.

"Brainstorm, share, converse, think it through…*Capiche?*"

Their hopelessness enraged me. I had problems of my own. This wall-eyed vacancy was the last thing I needed. A forced march into the heartland would get us nowhere. The campfire stories, sparking the imagination to flashpoint, didn't help much, either…

Disconsolate, but torn by guilt or by his obligation to stand tall, Mungo spoke first. The rivers of the Gambia were at peak tide, he said. We should, therefore, soon meet up with one of the many *coffles* (caravans) laden with chicory, spice and ivory, now crossing the jungle. Or we might encounter the Slatees. (Negro slave merchants, diviners, who flew across the continent on grand campaigns of mummery and malfeasance.)

In the clearing, our unsecured baggage baked like scones in the morning sun.

"This is our first common council," Caryn whispered. Enrique paused in deference, silencing for the moment the clamorous torque of his toe-drums. Maybe we were talking about him.

"Watch out," I said. "The Meema Taba will get you every time."

"Whazzat?" Caryn said.

"Only kidding. Meema Taba are large trees, draped with rugs. They indicate the presence of a well or a spring—"

"—or a wellspring…"

"...in the area. It is the local custom to hang a scrap of cloth on the tree's branch in honor of the elemental spirit."

Caryn was crying. "What else do they hang?" she asked. "Where in God's name are we, Victor?"

She was upset. Hell: we all were. Enrique flashed a tootlhsome smile. as Rudel stepped closer to the girl.

"Mademoiselle, la carte nous dit que—"

"For God's sake, Bertran—say it in English! I beg you!"

Meantime, Mungo is absorbed by some fleeting transposition of cloud and sky, a dexterous tracing of God's infinite regret.

"Pardon. We must follow ze map. Follow ze map—and inqui-et not. *Ça va?*"

Books, almanacs, schedules of meteorology passed from hand to hand. Enrique grabbed one and tossed it directly into the dwindling flame. I choked, felt a wave of violent illness wash through me; then the nervous spell passed.

"Victor--?"

"Continue," I insisted. "I'm fine. Right as rain."

Rudel handed me a huge tome, bound in greasy morocco that tarnished finger, khaki, and soul. On the Borders of the Pygmy-Land. Ruth Stanley, author. (No relation to Henry M.) Creeping rot had half-destroyed the book. "The natives of the countries bordering on the Gambia may be divided into four great classes: the Feloops, the Jaloffs, the Foulahs, and the Mandingoes."

Two of these nations were notorious for homicidal glee. Cannibalism, too, more common than toothache!

The Foulahs preferred robbery to outright murder (we read.) Next to nothing was known about Feloops.

The tribal names were barbarous, swoon-making. Ms. Stanley

prescribed diplomacy, urged the utmost tact in the unlucky event of encountering any of their number…

So went the third day. Noon: a lunch of meat hash splayed on honied aloe.

Rudel wants to break camp, get on with it, move on.

We are in the heart of the African jungle, our senses reduced to animal stupefaction . All Caryn wants to know is where. The novelists and poets of our time can transform and transcend everyday life—but the jungle's reality is all too real, wretched excess in far too great abundance.

Build a raft. Passage by water. Mungo the civil engineer will oversee its construction. Meanwhile Caryn plaits a rope of thick 'jungle hair.' Enrique hops about, a Mexican jumping bean decked out in Bantuesque garb. The Gambia floodwaters at their seasonal high. Vaguely I recall my salad days, the safety and calm of the Oxbridge libraries. The Schoolmen wrote that action quells fear: so be it. We would act.

We're afloat. A balsam trapezoid barely held together by hemp separates us from the roaring drink.

Rudel at the prow, spyglass in hand, eye fixed resolutely on the horizon. The Negro superb at the helm. Matchbox yacht. The river bank, exploding with green, changes with uncanny rapidity. We flip through the soaked pages of a botany, but like madness, like delirium, the flora and fauna continually change.

Fifth day out. Or was it the second day?

Rudel is quiet, save for his occasional utterance to the dog-faced natives of these parts. Mungo insists we have traversed over

one hundred miles of African waterway. We greet his pronounce-
ments with indifference. We are lethargic, lost in our dreams of
clotted cream, scones. and afternoon tea…

The quibbling has diminished us, has reduced our spiritual
fuel. Differences over moot points of topography, gastronomy,
geology…all the books, even the Zoroastrian calendars, are
gone. We take our meals by rote, mechanically: zombies feast-
ing on scraps hastily gathered from infinite swamp. The constant
change—the hallucinatory variations in tree height, color, character of leaf—casts a hypnotic spell. Even that eventually palls.
Forget Mandingoes. We are entranced, stiff-limbed statues, stone
idols tending to mindless nautical-type chores.

We check the horizon for signs of life. Again the river widens.
At this point, meeting the Mandingo would be a blessed event.

CATASTROPHE.

The jerry-rigged craft whirled and tossed about, flung violently downstream at breakneck speed, each sally more destructive
than the last. Sea and sky overturn in a ludicrous mix of light,
swamp life and jungle rot. A tangle of thorny vine dares commin-
gle with Caryn's streaming hair, lovelier than ever in the pellucid
damp. We are tossed pell-mell yet again. We take on water, we
dip, we sway, we capsize. Beneath the stream's surface galleries of
fish eyes peer at us, mocking our puny effort to set things right.
Human, all too human…Gasping for breath, my weakened lungs
bellow weakly, barely making purchase on the foul air. Moments
later I clear surface. I watch forlornly as the broken craft hurtles
swiftly by, to a watery grave in the headwaters beyond.

Mungo, drowning, keeps his head bent low, treading water

the best he can. I stare in deep disbelief, a waterlogged terrier in pursuit of higher ground. In the near distance Enrique bears a prostrate Caryn on his massive shoulders—twin ebony Himalayas gleaming in the cruel jungle sun—to the closer shore.

Where was Rudel? A general cry arose, but to no effect.

A lone gazelle runs past.

Provisions lost, our hopes dashed beneath the Gambia's muddy waves. A jagged strip of canvas, its tatters almost beyond recognition, waves us a final *God bless*!

No weapons…Even worse, no change of clothes.

AND NO BERTRAN RUDEL! (Was the purple bunting already lowered in Bertran's beloved Brussels-land?)

Rudel's absence was obscene. First the terraplane, now this. We sorely missed the vainglorious Belgian, the unlucky otolaryngologist lost to jungle and swamp. We beat a scared tattoo, screamed and hollered his name in vain.

"He won't answer to his name," Mungo observed. "Cut him a new one."

Dumbstruck, thoughtless as beasts of the field, we arose as one man (and woman) and surrendered en masse to Mungo's idée. As a single voice our terrible shouting began anew.

"Victor Frankenstein! Victor Frankenstein! Victor Frankenstein!" we cried.

I scanned the sparkling river for air bubbles, torn pants, a water marked hat band—for any sign of the man. Nada.

This was not the cruelest blow.

Stalwart as an unshaken tree before gale-force winds, Enrique remained undaunted, unmoved, verging on the inorganic. He dealt with contingencies. We Europeans on the other hand were weighted down, freighted with the Rosy Cross, thumb screwed with the armatures of an impotent freemasonry pulling us earthward, down, down, down...

Things were getting simpler. There was only jungle; the night; there was our fear.

As I pondered the fate of Rudel, I was soon overcome by a kind of neurasthenia, a fatuous soul-sickness. I imagined Rudel drowned, eaten alive, starving to death on some infested jungle floor. I took a poor sleep, made a poor water as these and other images tossed about in my head. O Albion, O Oblivion...

FOUR BODIES lay breathing in broken cadence along an unnamed river's tributary. Hereford, still 'physically' present, dreams of rowing the Thames. He is about to enter a world halfway between this one and the next. He would gladly trade his ruined collar for a dry surplice, a heavily starched cassock...

Caryn Felice? Tigers loosed upon our benighted party would spare her life. She rests in the phantom embrace of a Nubian princeling whose eyes she does not yet know.

Mungo dreams of cantilevers.

The journalist dreams himself an Africa: an Africa reborn, an Africa refreshed and renovated, service industries stretching as far across the savanna as the eye can see. He is walking now, tusk in hand. Pith helmet secure, his heart singing *Victoria, Victoria*...a crackbrained child tapping a makeshift drum wrested from his sorry cataract soak...

Kafir country. Mumbo Jumbo land. This arbiter, this minister of local justice (soon to be Hereford, whether he will or no), disguised in the abominable dress meant to replace fear with *lèse-majesté*, emboldened by a mask part beast, part manioc... armed with the rod of public obeisance, at last makes his approach.

Scepter in hand, Hereford begins. The pantomime is on.

He sashays to the bentang around which the others already sway in time.

Corrugated faces. Proud flesh. Mumbo Jumbo shits himself. The high stink carries on the breeze. The stench flushes a mountain lion out from its lair. Mumbo Jumbo's grass skirts are ca-ca-streaked, doubly- and trebly-soiled.

Every married female hopes that he's here for her. Sweet. They cannot refuse the summons; something custom will not allow. Mumbo fixes his zealot's eye on a woman just past her prime—she is perfect for him, just the thing! His arm, ringlets to the elbow, snakes forth, an uncoiled adder roused from its lair.

His dart strikes home. The woman called Jatta shrieks. *Tobabauo fonnio! Tobabauo fonnio*! Her eyes go strabismic, lose their gaze. She is seized, stripped, tied to a post. Then she is scourged with Mumbo's hot rod, with Mumbo's supernatural shrieks. She is impaled on her dark ancestry, on the misdeeds of her many previous lives.

Daylight puts an end to the indecent revel.

Meantime, a family of macaques has made short work of the now-forgotten terraplane...

Dutch, you write as though the Boer War were a
fiction whipped up by some malarial expatriate
hack; as though Swaziland were still an emerald
in the British crown, as if plate-lipped virgins still
shimmied through Bwana's moist dreams. Shame
on you. How politically incorrect!
    I see this work lavishly illustrated, easily mistaken
for a Chinese takeout menu. By all means, keep writing.
Lulu

Chapter 29

Rand

Who was it—Leon Trotsky, Sigmund Freud, Professor Irwin Corey—who asked, 'What do women want?' I found myself asking the very same question. My first wife, a psychiatrist, was a saucy little number, a hellion who stayed up nights with me killing joints, dead soldiers, as we listened to Coltrane and made fun of the world. Laughing until it hurt. Mondays were rough. Mondays we had to work.

She grew up in Monterey, the sole issue of a flash in the pan artist, a portrait painter, who eventually drowned in booze…Her mother, a Guinevere who favored flowing chiffon gowns. She quoted extensively from the *Morte d'Arthur*, from memory, in sexy cigarette-ruined tones.

Donna. She was from Monterey, a light drowned world, A dream world where horses ran free, where Irish wolfhounds galloped the spray on Carmel's silky strand. What did I know of such things? Not much…but it didn't really matter. We got on.Brainy New York Jews were her thing. The elective affinity was reciprocal: that strange galaxy of hers worked wonders on me. Never before had I celebrated midnight Mass, never before had I heard the Requiem through. Never before had I attended receptions where dry martinis were the main (and only) course. Black tie affairs went down smooth. So did the Quaaludes and her best friend Maxine. One memorable night we three menaged...I was happy as a clam. when they decided to go at it, two-on-one, with happy as a clam me. Granted, the after party was strange. We pledged eternal love, eternal fealty, under the stars of another beach—Montauk—emptying our blood into a silver chalice secretly purloined for the momentous event. With spondees and quatrains from Aleister Crowley, we pledged our astral troth, we fucked our brains out in the on call room at the prestigious university hospital, borrowed three dozen roses from the bedside of a dying patient in order to decorate ours. (They were no use to him.) Two dozen red roses marking the still warm sheets where I had pounded and squeezed and emptied myself into her perfectly lithe body.

Imagine my consternation...Donna took to depression, like a fish to water. A bit remote, a tad slack-jawed...definitely down in the mouth. Her new found despondency went on for weeks.

I tried to find out why. Was it her time of month? Was it the 'anniversary' of her mercurial dad's demise? Did she have an issue with success? We were hip yuppie *arrivistes*. I thought we were happy, our day job curing souls at the prestigious medical center...Why the frown, clown? Have mercy, Miss Percy! Why the sneer, Mynheer?

CHAPTER 30

THE HOUSE OF THE DEAD

How sad, watching a man rot in prison. How sad, watching a man with nowhere to go but down, clasping a well-worn copy of Magic & Mystery in Tibet to his heaving, careworn breast.

The prisoner kept a journal.

I write from an airless room in Madrid. My body is fettered to this time and place but my soul has wings. There is a Jack London story—who can give the name?—about a prisoner in a tower who makes the best of his fate by learning to quit his body.

The Art of Astral Projection. The Art of Mental Science & Hygiene. Harvest pure thoughts, then leave your body behind. Astral projection. So be it. The horizon an unbroken line but for my knowledge of the digital nature of the sight. They say a house fly can see a thousand times more detail than you or I. Dung beetles have five million lenses in each eye. For what? I am working on a device, a kind of time machine, that would freeze the retinal image at the time of death. These wavering fractals, these cold and unfeeling pixels, hold the key to the soul's highway. They hold the last thing on earth that any man sees. I know a guy who keeps a museum of these. I want to kill him but first I need the collection. I need to learn how and what to see. On second thought, I don't. I'll know it when I see it. It's good to think about the retina. Think about the vitreous humor, the jelly behind the incredible logistics of sight. Take the high road. I WILL NOT shit my pants. Does it really matter? One gal collected famous last words from the condemned of the Bastille. After the heads were severed they kept on talking: "Fuck you." "Take a hike, Mike." "Why the sneer, Mynheer?"

The prison chaplain, Victor Rand (a common name in these parts!), encourages me to write.

"It's not about cleaning up your act. It's too late for that. I'm here to help you write."

This Victor—a loser if there ever was one— says, "Let a smile be your umbrella,'Buy American!'"

I'll come back and haunt every last one of you. I'll hunt you down. I'll lead a mutiny in heaven. You haven't heard the last from me. Mark my words. I am and always will be a permanent part of the show. That's not a cloud on the horizon, that's me.

THE PRISONER had several sessions with the ward medic, also named [Dr.] Victor Rand. The medic had the same name as the chaplain but the prisoner was too tired to care. This arrangement was as convenient as any other.

The prisoner asked Rand, S.J. for a copy of the bible…and for the complete works of Jules Verne.

'Doc, I can't be brief.'

Given the circumstances, this could be a problem.

'Go on. And take your hands out of your pants.'

'If you insist.'

A beat.

"Hold me to the bare minimum. Hold me. I have a fear of death that creeps on every night. I know I won't die soon but then again I might."

"You're like water down the drain, just wasting away."

"Like plagiarism...Doctors can't help me, ghost of a man, that's me..."

"Hah!"

The priest jabbed the penitent's belly.

"Throw away that copybook. Write from the heart."

"Okay. This particular relationship—"

"Your marital journey—"

"Stop interrupting. This particular marital journey was not about you, fuck face. It was about belonging. About not having a home--not belonging anywhere."

"I hope you're past that. You'll always have a home in here." Rand, S.J. beat his breast.

"I had no voice. I took correspondence courses. I had a terrible thirst for recognition."

"Terrible thirst?"

"Unslakable. As in Nordhoff and Hall. Thirst is a metaphor."

"Precious..."

"No one really cares."

Silence.

The prisoner shot a murderous glance at the other man.

"Care to disagree?"

"I care..."

"Stripped of my attachments, of all fellow-feeling..."

"Walking the spiritual plank."

"Then there's the loneliness. The terrible loneliness. The jeers from nowhere. The phantoms who would laugh at you except they are silent, insensible. Are they or are they not?"

"More shadow than substance."

"A mere bagatelle."

"Vapid."

"Telluric."

The prisoner stole a glance at his watch. He didn't have time for this.

"I'll try again: a non-elective mutism clamping a steely muzzle on your heart."

"Now say it in English."

"Excuse me—?"

"I drift from puddle to puddle, setting off in five directions at once. I quit Miami. I abandon Madrid. I only visit cities that start with the letter 'm.'"

"You felt alone."

"Everyone in love but me."

"Wise up. Everyone's in love with you."

"I feel better already. May I kiss you? May I kiss your hand, Monsignor?"

The soldier of Christ did a double take, shifting nervously in his seat. The prisoner studied the cleric's Romanesque nose.

"Please. Call me Monsignor."

The prisoner grimaced.

"Walk a mile in my shoes."

"No thanks, my son." The minister reciting in Latin…

"Pure gonadal bliss."

"I'll take sex over stir-fried any day."

Another pause; another beat.

"I feel your pain. Now get the hell out of here."

"Pistil and stamens."

"Pistol and brass knuckles."

"Young bodies clutching, grasping, sharing a mindless frenzy of world-promotion. The biologic imperative. Even dung beetles lose themselves in the pursuit of persistence. Procreation."

"Better to shoot your wad...than shoot the priest."

"Well said. Now leave."

Chapter 31

The Big Night

'Twas the night before the big event. He puts the idiot box on—a talk show, a comedian who spits as he talks, who wets himself to the jeering pleasure of the studio audience. Then he decides against. Too much applause. Rand tosses and turns in his failed effort at sleep. He considers a sleeping pill but then decides against. His has to be razor sharp. Clear. Finally he drops off to sleep…rolled and tossed in nightmare's turbulent sea.

Maybe this is the worst of it. A little insomnia, a forward step all the same.

Death row. King Sol and Marcel Duchamp in cameo roles: his cell mates. Great company! Aleister Crowley too. Who could ask for more? In the other cell, a makeshift closet no larger than an oven, Franz Bardon paces back and forth, agonizing in solitary confinement.

The warden's keys clang and rattle, terrible sounds echoing down the long corridor. Even the concrete has a horrible smell—fecal, mildewed, anointed with the fragrance of terminal fear. No disinfectant could wash the ammoniacal tang away. Marcel bolts down key lime pie, Borges a modest glass of wine.

Rand once rented a lovely summer home. The owner, in a fit of largesse, left a tiny card. Welcome, it read. Enjoy your stay.

What a bad father he had been. Here he was with his heroes but he couldn't help himself. He had surrendered. Let him down. It was definite, beyond dispute. Rand would not enjoy his stay.

CHAPTER 32

BARDON'S STORY

BARDON, A MONGREL OF A MAN, had practiced occultism outside, in the beautiful vanished world. Bardon could be florid, paranoid, insisting that his ideas were borrowed, stolen, copied. He would not—could not—shut up about astral vendors, about psychic entrepreneurs who had stolen his thunder. More than once Crowley pulled a knife on him. This is why he was kept apart.

"A legend in my own time," he said with great bitterness. "A legend in my own time."

Bardon, like so many penny ante charlatans, was an inveterate liar. Like many Christian mystics he grew up in the Bronx but insisted it was Transylvania. Or the Black Forest. The Delaware Water Gap. Rand couldn't keep track. None of that was Rand's problem. He had other fish to…fry.

Bardon's whining was incessant. Here he was, within arm's reach of other potential initiates, yet he could not stop the clamor, could not staunch the bleeding of his sorely broken heart. Bardon's physical vehicle (his body!) was no place for a soul as ripe and numinous as his. He had worn out his welcome as a minister in Bavaria, getting his students pregnant in order to advance the cause of progressive metempsychosis. Bardon dreamed of wrenching a superior soul from beyond, dreamed of custom installing it in the body of a beautiful village woman.

THE PRISONERS converse fiercely, especially at night.

The prison guard turns a deaf ear to the clamor. He expects no less: after all, he has spent a lifetime listening to the ravings of the condemned.

King Sol also hails from the Bronx. Maybe that explains his vehement opposition to Bardon's freewheeling Slavic talk.

Bardon tears open his shirt and bellows, like some carney from hell.

"Step right up, right this way!" he shouts to the walls. "The miracle of magic! Look ma, no hands!"

King Sol, whose real name is not Sol Jesse Rayfield, but Sol Duane Berman, attempts to engage the older man in conversation.

Bardon turns pale. "When I was on the stage circuit—in Germany—they had to turn people away at the door. Everyone was there! I was in my heyday—even after the black shirts arrived. They called me Lucky. They called me Ace!"

"Lucky." The contempt in Crowley's voice cuts the moment like a knife—a dull knife, in rancid butter. But that won't stop King.

"It got to the point where an honest magician [sic] couldn't ply his trade. Couldn't practice in public."

"Practice?"

"Legerdemain," King Sol explains.

"Bastards," someone else pipes in.

"Gangsters," Bardon agrees.

Rand is puzzled by this.

"If you did practice—when they let you practice—what exactly did you do? What was your act?"

"Go ahead, laugh," Bardon says. "At the time it wasn't quite so funny. Freemasons. other practitioners of the mystery traditions…you left the country or you were shot."

"Hitler was widely known as a member of the 99 Lodge."

"Wrong," King Sol says. "Hitler was chief magister of the Aryan Order of Thule." Careful. This kind of talk could lead to a visit from the turnkey, to unkind words and a drubbing from the warden's nightstick.

"Listen up. You can laugh all you want. Laugh till you're blue in the face. What happened to me shouldn't happen to a dog."

"One of my students blew the whistle. Both of us were arrested and thrown into prison, thank you, back in '42."

"Arrested? Imprisoned?" Crowley feigns astonishment. "What happened to your psychism? What happened to your Magick, just when you needed it most? Couldn't have any of this been foreseen? As in foretold, avoided, predicted, my dear Nostradamus?"

"My disciple," Bardon patiently explains, "lost all control when he was flogged. His Qabalistic formulae did him no good at all. They took him out back, lined him up against the wall and one two three he was a dead man. They shot him."

"*Et tu*, Brutus?" (Duchamp was still thinking about his Pekinese.)

"Hitler offered me a position high up in the ministry. He was willing to let me live, on the condition that with my powers I would bring the war to a speedy close."

"Full benefits, sidecar, expense account too?"

"Schickelgruber—sorry!—Adolf—wanted me to speak against my brothers. *Natürlich*, I refused."

"Here comes the not so nice part," King Sol says.

"The gangsters tortured me. They forged iron rings. They soldered an 80 pound ball and chain, wrapped tight around my foot."

"For this there was no magic," Crowley sneers.

"That's not all, folks," Bardon says.

"There was more trouble. After the war I was back in stir again. The Czech authorities. They weren't keen on hermetic practice. They were jealous of my psychic prowess, of my uncanny ability to heal the sick...right the wrong..tell the good from the bad."

"*Natürlich*..."

"I cured my own cancer! Yet the bookstores refused to carry my books."

Bardon pulled at one of the few remaining strands of hair on his head.

"Look sharp, boys."

Silence.

Duchamp, always the clown, had methodically tied each inmate's shoestrings to the other's.

"There is a way out."

Crowley shot to his feet, in the process slamming his head against the steel bunk and tripping over his doctored laces.

"Don't say it, Franz!"

Bardon ignores the other man's plea.

"We created our very own lodge. The Fraternity of Saturn. Our very own lodge."

"Not only that...Guess what? I just happen to have a transcript of a recent meeting." Bardon produces a remnant of foolscap that had surely seen better days...

Chapter 33

The Lodge

'The members of this sect transmit their secret gospel by shallow truths.'
—Anonymous

"...AND SHE WAS A VICIOUS PIG."

A thrill of approval fills the crowded room. These are his brethen, his brothers and sisters. They stare at him. He looks up from the page.

He continues reciting.

"Rebecca de Montherlant fell into my life. She was a jaguar. She was raised in California. She was not only an adversary but a true lactovegan."

"She hitched up with the very first guy that came along. He blew a fuse. He flipped his lid! That's when she came to me."

The man continues. His tale is accepted uncritically—unconditionally!— by the adoring crowd.

The next speaker is plumed. (Her plumage is botanical, not avian. Bromeliad.)_ The visual spectacle does not overreach. Then she grabs the mike.

"Beverly Mathews hated his job and it comes as no surprise when I tell you how much he hated his name. To this very day he carries a torch for me! Beverly is a fool. He will not put by for a rainy day. And I will not suffer the embrace of a fool."

The Winged One speaks next. (There are no inebriates among this crowd.) The Winged One tells a 'story.' The brothers and sisters are scribbling, taking down his filibuster in frantic haste.

The elders of the lodge are divided, fighting bitterly at core issues. Were they or were they not Rosicrucians? And the narrators: were they only buccaneers? Their stories ran askew, ran empty and deep, utterly devoid of meaning.

They inscribe the tirade in glyphs, in the flame alphabet, as their number diminishes during the course of the long night.

Absent a mystical solution, they are desolute, *destruit, désolé…*

Chapter 34

Wizards at Play

"What kind of nonsense is this?" Crowley bellowed. "Guard! Guard! A sodomist lurks about!"

"Hold your tongue, miscreant." Bardon is mighty steamed up.

"We have telluric fluid…magnetic fluid, too! We use condensers and magic wands…focus the energy. Don't force me to use it on you!"

Duchamp unzips his pants. "Nothing magic about this wand," Duchamp says.

"Shut up! I will not be silenced! I have special authorization from the warden—' here he waves the moribund document, that decaying sheet of foolscap, "—from the prison authorities."

"From the game warden too," says King Sol. He feels for the old man. Christ in Heaven, let him have his moment in the sun!

"The four elements," Bardon begins, "are identical to those in use by the alchemists of old. Fire, Water. Earth. And then there is Air. Akasha, the fifth prime element, subsumes the qualities of all the others. A magician is a technician, a master spirit forged in the athanor's heat—a technician who can combine and focus the elements to achieve the desired effect. Only those who orchestrate the elements within can master the elements without…"

"Don't get me wrong. This Path is no picnic! Adversaries

abound. Gnomes, sylphs, lemurians—all lesser beings—are forever vigilant, forever on the watch. Given the chance they will ambush you...Depend on it: they will destroy your soul."

Rand yawns. "The price of freedom is eternal vigilance." Someone famous said that. When would the plagiarism stop?

"Any cause, allied with sufficient desire and will, through application of the proper combination of elements, can and will realize any effect. This is what I call Magick."

Crowley cold cocks Bardon with the heel of his shoe. Bardon wheezes, pitches forward, slumping into an unmagickal heap on the cold prison floor. The ensuing slam—Bardon's head, concrete floor—does little to deter him from his waking dream. He is Magister, even Hierophant, to a college of hermetic aspirants. Provided they follow the curriculum—provided they pursue their lessons with fanatic piety —they will have perfect lives. This is the magick blueprint, the hopeless fairy tale, of which the comatose man dreams...The somnambulist's syllabus: focused breathing; transmutation of lead into gold; the charging of talismans, charms, of personal items (including fetishes for luck and for safety); the stockpiling of rituals; transmigration of consciousness; metempsychosis and levitation; polite introductions (handshakes and watercress sandwiches, a heavenly string quartet) to high ranking astral beings; astral projection; training in clairvoyance, clairaudience, and *éclair*; instructions for recruiting familiars and elementals; the construction of fluid condensers with *aqua regia*; and last but not least, long distance insemination of tombs, wombs and tapestried rooms.

The condemned men risk turning gray. King Sol, an especially kind soul, proves himself the most patient auditor of all.

He thinks about Rand, about Rand's phantom progeny while Bardon extemporizes about barbaric invocations and spells. Bardon's book was impenetrable; not just that, but the matters of which it treats—the Qaballah, the kabalah, the qa-ba-lah!—are beyond the ken of the average motorist. Of this there can be no doubt.

"Why the sneer, Mynheer?"

"Crowley," Bardon sighs, "you really are a low life."

"But sex magick is such fun!" Crowley vamps.

Now Rand knew: he was truly in hell. Crowley has somewhere come up with some pamphlets that he distributes with infuriating missionary zeal.

"Read after me, gents," Crowley says.

"My book is for ALL," Crowley recites. "I have written to help the Banker, the Pugilist, the Biologist, the Poet, the Navvy, the Grocer, the Factory Girl, the Mathematician, the Stenographer, the Golfer, the Wife, the Consul—and all the rest—to fulfill themselves perfectly, each in his or her own proper Way."

King Sol and Rand pray for the truncheon.

No such luck! Crowley spouts on.

"Postulate: MAGICK is the art and science of causing change to occur in conformity with Will…ANY required change may be effected by the application of the proper kind and degree of force in the proper manner through the proper medium to the proper object."

Duchamp interrupts. "Hold it right there, pal. If that's all true, how come our brother here caught a bum rap? He's got a standing date with the Last Mile. Murder one…"

Crowley ignores the surrealist's jibe.

"Every intentional act is a Magickal Act.

"Every successful act has conformed to the postulate.

"The first requisite for causing any change is thorough qualitative and quantitative understanding of the conditions.

"Every man and every woman has a course…Anyone who is forced from his own course, either through not understanding himself, or through external opposition, comes into conflict with the order of the Universe…and suffers accordingly.

"A man who is doing his True Will has the momentum of the universe to assist him.

"Man is capable of being and using anything which he perceives, for everything that he perceives is in a certain sense a part of his being. He may thus subjugate the whole Universe of which he is conscious to his individual Will.

"Every force in the Universe is capable of being transformed into any other kind of force by suitable means. There is thus an inexhaustible supply of any particular kind of force.

"Man's sense of himself as separate from, and opposed to, the Universe is a bar to his conducting its currents. It insulates and limits him."

How did Old Sparky fit in?

Duchamp spits on the floor in disgust.

Chapter 35

King Sol

He too was nuts. He deserved solitary as much as the next felon. They must have run out of space.

King Sol (*née*, they say, Solomon Jesse Rayfield) took liberties with his cellmates. They were his personal slaves, his phalanx of fools. Crowley vowed to cut out his tongue.

Chapter 36

Cruel and Unusual

During the final months, the authorities saw fit to grant Rand's final request. Rand wanted a secretary; Rand got a secretary. The guys on the cell block were jealous. Not everyone on death row gets a secretary of his own.

She arrived the next morning. Rand—who now called himself Rand (sic)— expected something else. Not a beauty queen, perhaps, but something at least vaguely female. This creature was tiny; she was tiny, she was grotesque, an ingratiating lapdog who lived in a world of her own. The creature's hair was bobbed—ironed, marcelled, tortured—the bangs parted, permitting a garish view of the sunken orbits. Such eyes: eyes terrible to behold, dark fiendish orbs whose negative gravity sucked in planets, galaxies, hope. Not only that: Rand's secretary dressed funny too. The creature was accompanied by a crate, a crate packed to bursting with garments, potpourri, effluvia.

"Cruel and unusual," Duchamp said.

King Sol lapsed into silence. Right then and there. The King had been threatening such a break for quite some time. His negotiations with the prison cook temporarily distracted King from his vow—but nothing could hold him back now. King retreated to the corner of the cell, craned back his head, fixing his absent gaze on the convergence of wall and ceiling he had studied thousands of nights before.

"What are you looking at?" Rand's new aide demanded. She adjusted something around her neck, then cleared her throat twelve times in rapid succession... She began to bray.

"Feel like talking?" she asked.

Duchamp snapped at the bait.

"I feel like talking. Consciousness is Calvary. Consciousness is crucifixion. Madame, I simply cannot bear this life."

"You poor man. How awful," the amanuensis declared. "I know what you need."

She sidled closer. Meantime the surrealist had bitten his thumb down to the bone. A night in the infirmity had to be better than this...

CHAPTER 37

MORE ABOUT GAIL

RAND DREAMT A HAPPY FAMILY. Gail invented torments to quash his dreams. She sent him letters—imaginary letters from his unborn sons.

"Read this" Gail said. "Read this and weep!"

"Hi Dad, this is Judas. Remember me—your son? Just wanted to tell you how happy I am…deliriously happy, beside myself with joy…now that you're out of my fucking life! You know, really… you annoy the fucking hell out of me. I'm sick of your ways… cheating on my mom! Sick of your gaunt death's head, sagging in boredom at soccer games. So many people—hell, everyone— hates you. We have lawyers, we have family: your family. You have nothing. No one told me to write this. Hear what I have to say: it comes straight from the heart. Let me say this: mother-fucker, you are not going to do this anymore. Do not fuck with me, understand? Do not fuck with us. This is it—my final word. We will not allow you to win. My brother, my mom and I will have a decent life. Goodbye."

JUDAS, the imaginary older one, came into this world tarnished, a pre-fab cargo of insidious challenge growing bigger and stronger with the passage of time. He was bright, he was sensitive, he was eccentric. The kind of kid whose obsessions —fire engines, sirens, father-hatred—ran riot, ruining everything else.

Judas at the playground: a juvenile Stalin ready to conquer the globe. Other kids on the see-saw, climbing the monkey bars? Intolerable. An outrage! Tears of frustration, deprivation, invariably came next. Want to get along with the pint-sized Führer? You had your work cut out for you. After all, the apple doesn't fall far from the tree. One made apologies for him. One understood him. It was, as they say, a matter of life or death.

RAND had it wrong. Gail Rachel's was a bountiful love. Gail Rachel loved herself. A flimsy carapace of sophistication her birthright. She had inherited her exoskeleton from Zach. And Zach's game was fear. Naked fear. Zach instilled a fear of outsiders, of the *goyim*, branded these gifts so deep that xenophobia—always in the guise of gut-wrenching, tree-hugging liberalism—became the family's way of life. Every time he installed a septic tank, Zach made baby then teenaged then grown-up Gail watch.

Gail Rachel knew her stuff. When the American rocket ship exploded, she forced Rand and the dog to watch. Gail Rachel was an autocrat. Gail Rachel's opinions were as plentiful as they were onerous. But she had so many...

She raised her voice. Again and again and again. She didn't have issues—she was a diva. Especially when it came to humiliation. Victor had long since lost count of the times Gail Rachel called his very own mother a cunt. Each new eruption only hurt more. She was expert at hating. Hating him. Her put downs, her hastily improvised *bon mots* were clay pigeons, practice shots in the penny arcade of her life. That's why Victor spent so much time in the car. The car was Rand's haberdashery, his convenience store, a Motel 6 where he could retreat, catch his breath, bolster himself the best he knew how for the next inevitable round of waste management.

She finally threw him out. Three weeks later he started with the phone calls. Begging her, pleading with her to arrange tiny moments when he might see the dog. Everyone was embarrassed. According to Gail, Rand was capable of anything. Orders of protection fell like rain. For seven years they treated him as a madman; an untouchable. Gail had everyone convinced: Victor was a lush; a wife abuser; an intractable ne'er-do-well; and most egregious of all, an incurable worm.

Victor asked Gail how she felt about swimming with minnows. Orders of protection falling like rain! How could Rand's supremely logical question constitute a crime?

He was out of that house, out of there for good. Now he was in the Big House, residing restively with other scions of the electric chair. There were days he never spoke. Days when no one called. Gail Rachel kept up the limbic vaccinations, instilling all who would listen with healthy doses of fear. Rand was a monster, a mutant, a miscreant...Rand was a freak!

CHAPTER 38

SEPARATION. AFFAIRS. DUTCH COURAGE.

NOTHING HELPED.

Rand, holed up in some obscure terminus down Orlando way. Orlando, his least favorite town. Somehow he passed the time. He wrote post cards.

Dear _________ : (he wrote)

I try to retain impressions of this fair city. This hub of civilization (immortalized by notables like Vincent Price, Henry James, Ben Jonson) is the only place to be. No shit! Orlando has a pulse of its own, a living beating pulse that accounts for the more or less continuous erotic frenzy of the citizenry–and goes a long way toward explaining the historic pilgrimages to Orlando of Averill Harriman and William Makepeace Thackeray.

Yours truly,
Victor Rand

Chapter 39

Prison. A further setback.

Rand surrendered. He had to trust someone. It was almost time to go.

Rand started confiding in the prison medic, the good doctor, Deutsche. All well and good, until Rand noticed the pink flyer staring out at him like a fresh wound from the pocket of Deutsche's filthy old coat.

'What's that?' Rand asked.

Deutsche feigned ignorance.

'I asked you a question, dick-head. What's that?'

Deutsche, with a look of terrible regret, handed over the pamphlet.

GET THE JOB YOU WANT!
GET THE GIRL YOU WANT!
    NOW YOU CAN HAVE IT ALL—
THANKS TO PROFESSOR DEUTSCHE'S CUTTING EDGE
BREAKTHROUGH IN MENTAL
HYGIENE AND SOUL WOUND CARE!

Rand thumbed through the leaflet.

"You make a strong case for mental science, Doc."

King Sol woke from a dream.

"Couldn't help but overhear you," he said. "Is it mental science—a dental appliance—or grand larceny?"

Chapter 40

Rand's Confession

The prisoner had some last words. No prayers, just more irksome invective.

"Okay, this is it. This is the big one. This is why I killed her...

"Gail cancelled our trip to Florida. She enjoyed adulterous relationships, none of which I could approve. She went out of her way to displease me. She took no interest in my work...but then again, neither did I!

"The police were on constant alert. I was considered an ogre, a menace, a threat to society. I was deprived not only of contact with the dog, but with all dogs. All children. Was I gay? One thing I know: I needed help. Lots of it! Stan Graf called me on my birthday—but I never called back. Always the first to blame. Idleness, pornography, crazy impossible dreams...Miscalculated my way to bankruptcy. My slide rule? Always bent! We had orders of protection, not sex. Other couples seemed so happy. Gail conceived a child by phone. She always picked the restaurant. Always chose the movie. She chose her husband's mode of exit from this cruel unfeeling world."

The warden glanced nervously at the guard.

"Vic, can we move this thing along? The governor's got a busy day ahead."

"She went crazy when I declined asparagus at some cousin's wedding in D.C. Claims I threatened to kill Mark…Trevor…Trey. Angrily rejected forkfuls of food in public. There's more. I was a bad uncle. Intolerant of her stable of paramours. I ruined her career. She played me. I hovered, reacting to each syllable as though gut shot, wincing at the thrust of the knife. I lived a life of fear, awaiting the inevitable: the unilateral decision; the unfavorable comparison; the inevitable reference to one or another of her paramours, lovers, friends.

"I found old postcards, love letters, intimate stuff that would blow your mind. Your mind? Anyone's mind. The best one? An unsigned valentine dated 1985, bearing the insufficiently cryptic message, 'At last!' Her bedroom, her office lined with photos—none of them of me."

"Does the prisoner have any [more] last words?

Vic flashes a maniacal grin at his interlocutor.

"Sure you want to know? Imagine a world of non-stop nightmare, dense with griffins, malign spirits and devils of every stripe. Imagine an alternate universe with everything out of reach.

"Welcome to my world! Welcome to the legion of lost souls: I count myself among them. Say hello to the legion of incessant flashback, of intrusive dreams without end. Once the brain gets into the nasty habit of flooding itself—of living in a Breughelian cosmos—it needs powerful help recalibrating its set point. What it doesn't need? What it doesn't need is electrocution at the hands of the state."

What it about Jersey that he ranted so? Rand divides his remaining time between chatting up the doc and reading about wife killers: like John List, of Westfield, N.J. List's mother lived in the attic. Was that important?

Rand needs clemency, or at the very least, peace of mind.

Not a lecture from Deutsche.

"Sit still," Deutsche said. "On my last trip to the islands I befriended the governor general."

Chapter 41

Flip the Switch

They turn on the juice.

Rand hallucinates a son, the good son, who might have comforted him, who might have said,

"Dada, when you left for work this morning, why didn't you wake me up and take me with you?

"Zach, is there any system of slavery more vicious or profound than that of the listener entombed in deadly conversation without end? No exit. Catalogues of bondage flashed through his overactive mind: the spouse wrapped in chains of sexual, financial, and social obligation… lovers trapped in the prison of their embrace…Zach, you were the cruelest libertine of all: a vagabond spirit choking on its own vomit, its logorrhea, trapped in the roiling precinct of its ever decaying flesh. All the alchemical woodcuts, the medieval torture-scapes, were etched by the same artist…The Tibetan Book of the Wed…Happiness Does Not in This Direction Lie. 'Lycanthropy is the obverse of misanthropy.'"

Rand wants a son who lowers his voice and says, 'I missed you so much.'

Chapter 42

Divorce. Separation. Death.

Together they roam a space of well worn vacuity. Speaking would only complicate matters, tarnish the hard won freedom of silence they have worked so hard to achieve these many years.

The woman's face had taken on a slate gray hue.

She moved in space and time with a curious look, a look of impassivity that could relapse any moment into tears or rage or choleric steam.

Their decade together: it could have been a century, or mere seconds—thousands of moments spent in pursuit of a language of gesture, only to abandon the hard won lexicon at a moment's notice, at the drop of a hat. The separation a violent scission, the violent fracture of the hybrid gamete fused in the fires of Hephaestus, the bisecting of the angel whose wings beat so gloriously so long as the price of partnership stayed cheap.

Now he spends entire nights on a wretched foam pallet, sequestered from wife and hearth in some other room. Vic balances clementines in one hand, three barges' worth of pain in the other. His was a radical realignment, a forced march, Bataan-like, a hideous wailing at the obsequy of some beloved yet newly killed king. Was the king just dead—or had he been crazy, too?

"Is there no hope?"

Gametes. That's all they were.

Mindlessly she recited the cost: social, financial, emotional.

What she had. What he didn't.

"We're throwing it all away."

And while they were throwing it all away, other couples were nesting, splitting logs, gluing the cerement, inscribing in cuneiform the piety of their sanctimonious lives.

NOTHING quite so soothing as the bluejay at dawn.

The laughter of the crow.

The perorations of a puffin.

The maunderings of a meadowlark.

The tintinnabulations of a titmouse.

The electric thrill of the chair.

Rand felt the talons of a congress of muskrats, marching single-file over his bare skin.

Ratiocination finally yielding to a Niagara of tears.

His new place would be ready soon.

This watershed period…the forced cohabitation…the tense mourning, his sexual absence from the world…All this left him weary, tearful, drained.Women were better at suffering; generally speaking, they got the better end of the deal. Sometimes it got so bad…that all he could do was wash dishes, boil water, do something, anything, to squeeze a placid moment from the squall.

THE GENERAL TENOR of things completely wore him down.

This life was definitely ending, was definitely on the wane— was there a new one to take its place?

His efforts at conversation were pathetic. Ineffectual. When it came to loose invective, Rand was shooting blanks.

RAND made it worse by reciting as if in prayer the litany of injustice that stayed his hand, jerked him off, pushed his buttons, yanked his chain and in a word compelled him to jettison everything he had and everything he knew—especially her.

HER DETACHMENT stung him to the core.

The worst of it? Had to be his feeble attempts at overture, at approach, his niggling efforts to bridge the chasm, essay a tentative negotiation between the two.

Times like this, in abject tenderness, in the deepest leap of faith, he would steel his nerves, gather his wits, muster the strength and courage to gather her up in his arms—their lips brushing, his pulse quickeng—and without fail he would pee himself gold.

She pulled away, jettisoning him in disgust. Rand was a cigarette butt, mindlessly flicked from the window of a moving car. A wholesale rejection of his being: her disgust as palpable as a punch to the gut. Lord, but it hurt! Did he want sex? Or was it only a hug that this heartsick remnant of a man coveted?

Sorry, no hugs. He would have settled for a shrug, settled for anything but having to watch her sleep: how could she sleep in the face of such pain?

"Can't we just be together?" he asked.

"At peace, side by side, now, at this point in time?" As if the question were insane!

"Your longing for me is inappropriate. It belongs somewhere else—in another place, another time—not here."

She aimed the remote, Glock-like, at the idiot box. She watched her shows.

Chapter 43

Marriage. A Near Death Experience

His only consolation was the near constant presence of a familiar, Felix Deutsche by name. Soon enough there would be another Deutsche, a real Deutsche—the latter a Julius—who would work on his head.

Rand had been through such things, and worse too!

Rand told his imaginary companion about his double failures in literature and in life.

He spoke of a double decline, of doubly lethal declensions in the world…Pick a point in time, his familiar advised. Any point. Any point will do. Begin at the beginning.

Gail had so many friends. Friends; attachments; infatuations; idolatries; idealizations that left Rand limp and wretched. I should have known this from the start.

I would never win her love. Never!

He steered a course just this side of sanity. His published self became his only self: Gail the harsh editor of the palimpsest that was his life. Time, fate and the very real prospect of a subtracted future left him impoverished, breathless.

Pass the bottle, Mac.

Rand started putting in time and a half at the human service agency.

He was nominated to a league of asylum superintendents.

Keepers of the societal flame.

His soul was consumed in the care of the marginal, the devout, the defective. He tended the ranks of the morally insane. (The term is not outdated. Moral insanity is very much among us, very much real.)

Words flowed like blood from the unstaunched wound that had once been his brain.

But then, unexpectedly, he thought, *Enough!* Rand had had enough. Enough of these fancies, these specters, these will-o-the-wisps conjured by the incessant rubbing of hairy, horny palms.

Rand went for help. He paid a parasite to refract his words, his wants, his wounds.

Doctor Julius Deutsch. Deutsche the polymath. First a career optometrist, then a counselor. Deutsch's office was on the second floor of a four-story walk up, right above the Chinese laundry.

Pistachio colored walls and the sweet clean updraft of starch.

The checks started coming in; Deutsch insisted he was blind. He would not see me [Rand wrote.] I had to write to him. At his lunatic insistence, we conversed in crayon.

He gave me a box of Crayolas, 52 identical crayons colored periwinkle blue. "Strictly a matter of taste," Deutsche explained. "You see, I'm color blind; periwinkle's the only color I see."

He forbade the use of carbon paper.

And he forbade the use of the letter R.

DR. DEUTSCH [Rand wrote], I compose these costive complaints from a prison cell in Miami. Untenanted, tossed from my room onto a garbage strewn beach somewhere on the Florida coast. In the near distance air ships frolic, practicing maneuvers among wisps of cirrus.

The fulfillment of all my dreams.

At Deutsch's advice (delivered in a crapulous tone by phone) I took a room that overlooked the bay. Palm trees listing in the predictable way. A storm could arrive. The ocean's blue skin. The horizon—no longer an alloy of sun, sky and briny foam—is ruined by the hulking presence of man. No, not man...a rigging platform. A terrible scaffold, its rusting scaffold loosing poison petrols upon once virgin shoals for miles around...

"Doctor," I said, "this is my hypertensive crisis. I've got pressure! Can you help?

"Doctor, I beg you: do not insist on brevity.

"Where is my home? Where do you go when you simply do not belong?

"And what of malaria? Getting on in years, in a forced uphill march? Then there's your pellagra, your glioblastoma, your heartbreak—of psoriasis?

"I am not, I repeat, not, a terrier. I have no sense of direction.

"I did not ask to be born, etc., etc.

"Which Rabbi, which Genius of metempsychosis, served up this plate of savories?

"When the meadowlarks lark, when the hoot owls hoot, the temptation, doctor, is to sing the praises of creation. But...there's elective mutism, voicelessness, a cogent thirst for recognition, wracking dehydrations—none of these strangers to me."

"No one cares what you think," Deutsch said. "Not even me. My fine-feathered friend, you have been summarily ejected from the throne, ingloriously stripped of attachments, bonds, shorn of fellow-feeling."

Insuperable loneliness. An arc of longing aimed for quadriplegia.

The riddle of sexual release at the hands of the day nurse.

Non-participation *mystique*.

Deutsch tells me to muzzle my heart.

Have a nice opthamologic (or urologic, the choice is mine) procedure.

From the motel room I dream a perfect Miami. I experience sleep inertia, apnea, paralysis. Erectile paralysis, too.

I empty my bowels on the floor, promptly notify the night clerk but he couldn't care less.

Sweethearts young and old, a never-ending spectacle of gonad-al bliss, stroll along the strand. Stamens and pistils, gonads, sex-crazed anthers clutching at each other, for each other, prodding and poking blindly in a world-promoting rapture of sleep. Sheer biology: the frenzy of procreation. I repeat: not for me!

DEUTSCH looked as if his greatest wish was to inject me, to plant an ice pick or weapon of similar effect in some crucial part of my brain.

Instead he just hung up the phone.

All of the heinous crimes that can be foisted on another have been committed—all in the name of holy consanguinity—against me.

The actual list of crimes bored the doctor to tears.

Once again, the actual list of crimes: defamation, moral deflora-tion, derogation, repossession, forced masturbation, price-fixing, emasculation, character assassination, devaluation, war-monger-ing, castration, betrayal, desertion, negligence—and let's not forget cruelty of the most abased and cruel degree. Imprisoning Martha Stewart belongs up there too.

My thoughts (sic) were interrupted by the phone. This time it was a man insisting that I speak with him in Spanish.

…This soul-crunching harridan, this chimera without wings, this juggernaut of ferocity whose shrewishness tumbled forth unaltered by self-awareness, she who has wholly stripped me, degraded me, (hurt my feelings, too), melted the wax of my dignity…a stereopticon of sobriquets, a strumpet's vomitus of venery and vilification…Gail's reptilian motives ever more arcane, ever more obscure…poisoning minds with her big-legged woman's ways…Her slander I could live with…but only by spitting out the worm whole.

The boy waits patiently to be born. Probably thinks of me as something feral, the grown and intransigent pup of Romulus and Remus that would diminish his mother, submit her to a course of distillation (yes, I have my stash of alembics), sublimation, transmuting the dross of her coarse matter into tasty London broil.

Surely this explained the arrival of the police in our happy home one night. I offered the fellow a dram. *Glenmorangie.* All I got for my generosity was a set of cuffs and a ride downtown.

'Sir', the good officer brayed, 'you must leave the house.'

'May I gather my belongings?'

In my haste I overfed the goldfish—fatally, I am sure—and as a result left the house skating on a river of tears. To this day my sorrow is bottomless; I still pine for the good true eye of that carp.

The police lights, flashing on and off like some apocalyptic rendering of Bosch provided a fitting and mete accompaniment to this shameful eviction from the nest.

Neighborhood kids were scared. My handkerchief, clutched between ball of fist and cuff, clotted stiff with fear, snot and nostalgia.

Visit the haberdasher, fool! I reminded myself.

Would that our home had been ruled by a fine Portuguese sardine, rather than by the fishwife who pretended to share my incomparable throne.

Chapter 44

Rand in the Manger

How many times he appealed to his Heavenly Auditor? How many times had he applied greasepaint to his Holy Guardian Angel?…Nonetheless the spectre's visage, not a pretty sight at best, was forever ruined by his—Victor's—bleak spiritual outlook. The only spiritual exercise (aside from those of Loyola) that gave him any lasting comfort was the contemplation of those he imagined attending his funeral and interment. Rand could not stop thinking about the day of his death. This was nothing new. As a child he had dwelt woefully and at great length upon the event. Rand's childhood years were tainted not so much by the premonition of his eventual passing as by a more or less general weakening—a dilution—of any possible future pleasure. When Rand learned that one could descry kabbalistic motifs in gangland slayings— could explain in profound spiritual terms the how and why of gangland-style executions—he momentarily brightened. He momentarily brightened at the thought. He championed the rights of gangland poets everywhere. Rand began introducing himself as H.P. Lovecraft's grandson but that carried little weight in the social circles he traveled in. Rand's best friend, an essayist, lived on white bread and awesome dollops of anchovy paste.

Chapter 45

Humble Origins

Victor Cornelius Rand (née Manny Radnitzky) was born in a flophouse on the Lower East Side of New York. His virgin birth was attended by a collegium of bums, bards, and beatniks. Rumor had it that Alan Ginsberg and Ferlinghetti presided over the occasion. Corso thought that was a 'crock of shit.'

In the next stall several chickens were either mating or being slaughtered. Pullet parts and feathers—a fowl *Grand Guignol*—flew apart in the airless space. Two stalls over a hobo was inscribing his life story on the toilet seat. When he ran out of blood he asked for a pen.

Tristan Tzara, the true and only presiding genius of the event, frowned with displeasure. His parsing of the latest John O'Hara (*Butterfield 8*, according to rumor) novel had been interrupted by the unwelcome arrival of this babe.

The motley gang gathered close to catch the infant's first words.

"Buy American," he cooed. He refused the proffered breast. No good: he wanted Meister Eckhart!

The obstetrician, borrowed for the occasion from his customary veterinary pursuits, ripped the latex glove from his working hand, turning his besotted attention to the swinging umbilicus. Which was pulsing and very rapidly turning blue. There was a vexatious quality to this pulsation, as though the newly minted matter was already enraged, already embittered, at the prospect of its cargo of tears to come.

A nursemaid was hastily appointed. This was a woman better left to herself. Her nervous tic worsened at the prospect of responsibility.

Nonetheless she took the infant in her dusky arms.

"My child," she mewled, "let me tell you about this terrible world."

She cleaned the weeping child with the last card of her tarot deck (it too had seen better times), flinging the bloodied sodden trump into the hayloft behind.

"I am a bride of the guillotine," she said.

The clamor had long since turned to din. No one wanted her to speak.

She held little Victor in the crook of her good arm, extracting at the same time a slim volume from the virtual space where once her breasts had been.

"Hmm," she pondered, applying her single apposable thumb to the rank pages of the book.

"My sweet lamb," she cooed, "*Mignon*…Ahh, here we go…" She flipped through the pages, as though capable of intentionality. "A short list of the Rosicrucian victims of the blade. And what each said at the moment of truth."

"Forget Buy American!" the newborn cried. "You're nuts!"

'There, there," she consoled, "don't forget my practice in midwifery—three decades in all, at the Salpetriere. I know whereof I speak."

From the back of the hayloft a sailor chimed in.

"Hey you!" he cried. "Don't shit yourself!'"

She had some choice words for him.

'This baby has yet to breathe! Everyone out! Clear out, I say!'

The crowd of drunkards, pederasts, soothsayers and mindless mages, hell bent on the favors of phantoms, roared their discontent.

The woman swung the child violently about.

"I can see it," she said. "The child wears the mark of the devil…Death…The Hanged Man…The Emperor…" She relaxed her stranglehold on the now quiet child, copping a look-see at the Infanta's tiny prick.

She found a whelk colony where his codpiece should have been.

"A sign from God!" she squealed.

Three more drunkards—Mexicans this time—staggered in.

"Where's the cockfight? We were drinking, out there on the campanile…"

Chapter 46

Rand Considers a Move. Too Much Poe

As the shades of evening drew on I at length found myself within view of the melancholy House…With my first glimpse of the building, a pervasive gloom rocked my soul. I thought of my dream girl, Gail Rachel, and of the glorious future that would surely be ours. She had vouchsafed her heart to me and here I was, trampling on its hedged precinct, destroying that which I did not yet own.

Gail was up most nights, crafting love letters to me in her delicate hand (or dismissing me forever from her thoughts.) The germ of infidelity had taken root in the fertile tissue of her mind and she now practiced betrayal a hundred—nay, a thousand—times a day. Her discontent was of the constitutional type and therefore not subject to influence. Her inner stirrings were unrelieved by any poetic sentiment with which the mind usually receives even the sternest images of the desolate or terrible. She worked that pussy with a ferocity and intensity of purpose awful to behold. Now she looked at me with an utter depression of soul. After sex she would drift off, Ophelia-like, gradually taking on a spiritual vacancy, a languor that left me high and dry.

The moment I came she was out of the bed, dragging the jismed quilt to the basement for another spin in the dryer. I felt used, used up. I thought of myself as a mote, a nothing, as the after-dream of the opium smoker. Gail experienced me as a bitter lapse into banality, into the common life—as the hideous dropping of the veil. Before we married I had tried but failed to commit her hand to a prenuptial contract of *suttee*. No way! There was an iciness, a sinking, a sickening of the heart—an unredeemed dreariness that could not be transformed into anything other than what it was. Perhaps Gail could find happiness with another man; another mansion; another strip mall. But it was too late to turn back. I had given the bum's rush to my last girlfriend (also called Gail.) All I had now was the gray sedge and the ghastly tree-stems, and my nostalgia for Gail.

Deal with it, sez I. We had cucumber sandwiches and tea. Friends came by to commiserate. I bought her pets. Gail quickly tired of these, let them lay fallow, without food or drink for weeks at a time. I was at my wit's end. I called upon her old flame (for whom, for all I knew, she still carried a torch.) I begged him to do what he could to rekindle her flagging spirit. As it turned out I would pay a heavy tariff indeed for her former consort's time. His family had a peculiar temperament. His devotion to musical science doomed the tranquility of our home.

Her former lover came to stay. Not only that, but decided that he could remedy Gail Rachel's familial deficiency of collateral issue. The burning question for the gentleman turned out to be whether to screw my wife on the table or on the baby Grand.

Meantime Vlad Tepesch, a Rumanian advocate whose services I had recently had cause to hire, asked us to join him at bowling. I would have, were it not for Gail Rachel's pseudo-consumption. My childish experiment—of looking down the tarn—quickly led me to a grove of cypress and just beyond, to a convenience store. Burdened with the ontology of choice, I zoned out, dissociated to a realm where real estate, land parcels and strip malls were meted out first come, first serve. This was a place which had no affinity with heaven. The dead and dying trees stank, emitting an inelastic vapor that dispatched the sparrows and pigeons unlucky enough to wander into their terrible toxic zone.

Vlad, now at my side more often than I might have wished—always ready to bill me for his time—added greatly to my discomfort. *The meter is running, man.* I begged him, pleaded with him—not so much for my sake as for Gail's—to lay off. Such is the law of all sentiment having terror as its basis. Back off bub! Hurl your faecal bastinadoes somewhere else!

Gail Rachel...Medusa...Helen of Troy. Where would it end? Where does a creature of addictive appetites go, but from this life to the next? Bummer...

The room in which I hung myself was huge.

I survived the event.

Ever so weary, Gail at last rose from her loveseat and stood beside me as I dangled before her in space. She had applied tincture of belladonna to her eyes to impart a false expression of concern.

"Darling!" she spouted.

That's when I screamed. "One step closer and I will kill myself!'" I threatened.

She was unmoved by this. Instead, she offered me a cordial.

"Some epinephrine, darling? Or another taste of the lash?"

She would not take me seriously. I asked for witnesses, asked for a general alarm to be sent throughout the house. Vlad, my neighbors, even our houseboy Glen, might have some feeling about my suicide.

"You reek of the charnel-house," she said. "Everyone knows this is nowhere."

Chapter 47

Relo

Rand had to move.

He scanned the real estate page but could only hear music. The print hovered, quivered, like tiny flaming letters. The damn ads were in Hebrew!

Rand lacked French, Spanish, Greek, and Hebrew. (Since when was the real estate printed in Hebrew?)

Now he was bathed in sweat.

Shit. What if the prison is in Hebrew, too?

Rand took the phone. The operator…

"Real estate agency, please."

"Which town, sir?"

Must there be a town?

"Sir…?"

Connected at last: the agency. The broker's voice grew friendlier the more desperate Rand's became. Alcatraz or the affluent suburbs: those were his choices.

So the very next morning Rand signed his life away. He pretended he was single (anything to get through this.) The new place would be nice, he thought. It could probably tolerate any amount of discord. Any place he chose would be great, no?

Rand's prospective neighbors greeted him with gusto. Not so

much innuendo as shit-faced bonhomie. At least he would have some friends.

Boots—that was the guy's name—explained about the kid.

"Challenged, very challenged...."

Boots nodded, indicating the shed right below Rand's apartment-to-be. "Down there, man. You're down there."

"Oh yeah," Boots now remembered. "One other thing."

Rand returned a look of defeated civility.

"I drink. A lot."

Boots' wife approached Rand, bearing a tray on her deeply bruised arms. How nice. Our very first meal. How nice, the bagel halves piled like discarded Michelins round a cup of steaming worms.

"Night crawlers," Boots explained. "Wendy's big idea."

Don't tremble. Be gracious and accept the meal.

Rand's hostess set the hor d'oeuvres down and winked slyly at him.

"Care for a drink?"

Boots poked Rand in the ribs.

"Hey brother, coffee, tea or me?"

Whatever Boots had taken that day was still coming on, still going strong. Otherwise, Rand suspected, the social niceties would have long since given way to broken teeth, limbs, even worse.

"So Vic, what line of work you in?"

I actually work, he wanted to say.

Wendy served her husband, slathering the spread around the bagel with a hunting knife. She finished, patted her hands on her thighs, and offered Rand the lease.

Boots picked at his teeth. Something vitreous, but still alive, came flying from his opened mouth.

"Any questions, dude?"

Boots reached for his wife and took her hand. She fidgeted then surrendered to his touch.

Wendy stared hard at Rand.

"Tell him about the fights."

"Quarrels," Boots said. "Not fights. Quarrels."

Rand signed the form and handed it back.

"Just so you understand, Vic. Care for a drink? Do you hunt? Like heavy metal? I'm sure your kids will love the place."

Rand could hardly wait to move in.

"So attracted to her you were? Someone put a gun to your head to sign the lease?" Incrimination, the suffering of the fool, and then the balm of Gilead. "Don't worry. It's not too late to back out."

Rand, stammering again to a faceless and for all he knew remorseless broker on the phone, explained that he needed a place. Not a girlfriend, not a bagel…just a humble roof to cover his head. Someplace kids might like. An alternative (he kept this last remark to himself) to Murder One.

Should he move…or should he murder? Homemaker or homicide?

Victor weighed the options. Maybe he could wait. On the other hand, with sufficient time, marble and skill, he could fashion a Laocoön…No trucks or leases needed for the Big House. And the Big House came furnished.

So Victor moved on, canceling that last check and meeting

post haste with prospective landlord numero *deux*. Rand could tell right away that the man had been altered. Terribly altered. Bald, deep strip mining of the fragile facial flesh, craters like the astronauts pretended to find on the moon. The fellow's face put Rand immediately in mind of rape: the rape of Gaia. Only his eyes moved—furtive, paranoid—an ineffectual mimicry of what usually passes for social intercourse. The man's legs, his body, the book in his lap—unmoving, each frozen in place. Moral vacuum? What else could it be: a surfeit of shelled pistachios?

Still, Rand liked the place. After all, it was a mansion, a mansion with rooms beyond number. The lawns needed professional care. Good. Rand could not be blamed for his choice.

LATER, over drinks, his new landlord Franz explained his vast wealth.

Franz was seventy-three. His mother had inherited the house. The inventor Thomas Edison had given it to her, as a gift, as a means of placating her—a misread and bitterly recalled amatory gesture. The inventor had had a string of affairs, including several 'white nights' in Albany that had set tongues wagging. No good! Take the house and call it a day.

THAT was a time when Edison the man was flying. The ideas poured like molten steel from the flaming crucible of his brain.

Grandma became heavy with child the very same week Edison invented the electric chair. Imagine that!

Clothide—Grandma—had been quite a girl.

Franz explained the terms of his new tenant's stay:

You have the run of the house, except where we live.

You can run around naked if you like. You can come and go as you please.

Two months into your stay you will find your belongings sniffed, riffled, gone through; your windows perpetually closed; your every movement tracked and recorded on the mainframe computer I keep in cold storage in the basement of this house. Where that is is no business of yours, my friend. Under no circumstances may you use the basement or garage.

No one in this house eats.

My father Leonard invented the self-cleaning toilet plunger. We are a family of inventors (if you don't believe me, ask the IRS.)

My grandmother slept with Thomas Edison. That's how we got the house.

If you fool with the wiring you run the risk of electrocution.

Don't bring any girls here.

Any questions? Good.

And please: enjoy your stay!

CHAPTER 48

NOSTALGIA

THERE WAS A TIME when Gail was considered quite a catch.

At the moment, however, she was going through this insufferable Pat Benatar phase. Her hair was hennaed, down-pointed, Peter Pan pixie-like.

She was starting to sag but she still got away wearing tank tops and those low cut skin tight jeans. Rand watched her bend over, watched Gail tending to the rutabagas or compost or last week's dog poo. Gail Rachel bending over, fetching something from the sink, troweling their modest garden. His antipathy was not yet universal; he could still appreciate the inviting crack of her tightly denimed ass. Her hips flared too…the butt had a fullness to it that was something new. It wasn't there when they were courting, when Rand strummed villanelles like a heart-sick jongleur crooning from garden to casement above. Now she preferred heavy eyeliner, deep dark mascaras, preferred heightening her semitic look. Turkish, Middle Eastern, Aramaic…the bitch had huge eyes. And they got larger every day. Gail had anger, love, slow-acting poison, all kinds of traps in those eyes. The eyes were humus brown, intelligent in ways she didn't even know. Gail's eyes carried the lineage, bravura and martyrdom of 5000 years of pain. Such talent! Such beauty!

Rand enjoyed the gradual settling and lowering of her breasts over the years. He heartily approved. These orbs were big to start with. They never sat all that high on her chest. Half the month they were pillowy, creamy. The rest of the time they were firm (if not fibronodular) with a fullness that helped dilute his atheism. Gail's rack was something to believe in. Her undie collection was nothing to sneeze at either (particularly for a quasi-fetishist like Rand.) The scanties were black, red, ablaze with leopard spots. Sometimes he had to look away. Her underwear put him through changes…rocked his paraphiliac world!

Hell: better to dispatch her, better to take care of business, then tarry much longer in this phantom grove. There would be other girls, other Wonderbras. The thin straps, the twists and turns and breath-taking incursions of fabric, that wondrous hinterland of thigh and pussy…after prison there'd be more. He could always dream…

He felt bad for Gail Rachel. She expected to be treated like a girl. Didn't they all? She had pleasant moments, nanoseconds of tenderness: girl things, girl moments, girl times. Why couldn't she get with the program? Why did she have to die?

Did she really need to die? Was her death necessary because of the collective hostility of the Berensteins, the Goldsteins, the O'Malleys, the Mullers, the Jacobsens, the Lanskys, the Kaplans, the Teitelbaums—towards him? Or was it because every hook-nosed creature in Gail's circle had been tutored in the same school of hate?

"You're a freak, Victor Rand, a freak," she said. "Go ahead, deny it."

RAND quit his post at the agency, more or less confining himself to the surprisingly narrow and airless perimeter of the 18 room mansion.

He collected everything he could find on the subject of succubi. Demonocacomania. Intercourse with demons. The biblical Lilith. The sapping of the male vital fluid...

Samson and Delilah. Lycanthromania. Psychic vampirism. Creatures who fed on the spiritual essence of others. Rand knew of a priest in Prague (or was it a rabbi?) who could exorcise such things. Sure. Right away. Let's go.

FRANZ'S WIFE, Natasha, his landlady-in-arms, slipped up the stairs on the soundless soles of her bunny rabbit slippers. She had a way of floating, of getting in Rand's face, that deeply unnerved him.

"Victor," she said, "look at me."

Her Byelorussian face, that face with its Kirghiz eyes, had lost its customary softness. Now her skin was mottled, angry, red. Her eyelids were swollen, hugely swollen, looking for all the world as though they might shut down for good.

"Poison ivy," she said with oracular authority. "I need help."

Late afternoon and she was already in peignoir. What kind of help did she have in mind?

"Should I send for Franz?"

Natasha winced. No. Calling her husband was a bad idea.

"No, Victor—I need a doctor."

Rand threw down his pen. Franz had spelled it out right from the start: no privacy in these quarters. Rand's manhood stirred momentarily then retracted, intraperitoneally, as deeply as it could.

"It's true: I'm a doctor. But I'm busy," Rand said. "Terribly sorry."

She turned away. The silk and satin and abhorrent wheals were gone.

THE UNAPPRECIATED ROLE, Rand wrote, of succubi and incubi in the rapid deterioration of modern life will wreak havoc with any efforts on the part of society to progress beyond mere survival. All it takes is one psychic remnant, one malign spirit, to cannibalize the remainder of an individual's personality and physical and spiritual well being.

LANDLORD FRANZ apologized for Natasha's intrusions.

"You know who lived here, don't you?"

Franz gazed at him with reptilian (lizard relaxing on a hot rock beneath the sweet rays of a warm sun) detachment. Rand felt like a fly, a paramecium, like the weekly tonnage of cut lawn that disappeared from the manse with frightening regularity.

"I can't imagine," Rand said.

"Kafka. Vincent Price. And the American writer…Ben Jonson."

It was obvious, transparent, clearer than ever before: the sooner Rand did the crime, the sooner all this would go away.

"Ben Jonson, you say. Perhaps you meant Al Jolson?"

Franz was offended.

"You don't like Ben Jonson? You don't like my wife?"

AMUSEMENT PARK NIGHTMARE. Mother of Two Falls to Death from Ferris Wheel in Front of Horrified Onlookers. Jersey Joy Ride. Mother of Two Tumbles to Death: Accident or Murder One?

Victor Rand, Alcatraz-style, raps to the prison doc.

"Can anyone blame me for straying? I went outside the marriage in the innocent pursuit of love."

"Get any?" Julius Deutsche, the prison psychiatrist, asked.

"Love. Love and tenderness."

"Fess up: what you really want is pussy." And if that was not enough,

"You did the crime, you do the time."

Ouch. This is what they paid Deutsche for?

Rand tried again.

"These surrogate jousts, these empty perorations against an uncaring universe, left me with at least a foot hold in the land of the living."

Deutsche found this particularly funny. Deutsche roared with laughter, with mirth, with window-rattling approbation.

Rand suddenly remembered the cheesy-looking pamphlet, the sullied paper ground into near unrecognizability by the heels and toes of countless passers-by. The palimpsest-what was left of it—read:

GET THE GIRL YOU WANT!
GET THE LIFE YOU WANT!
YOU TOO CAN HAVE THE
PERFECT LIFE!!!

Rand's pen, a dime store throwaway, kept running out of ink.

Did they have fountain pens in prison?

Arguing the case for mental science...Was it mental science...or grand larceny?

Gail's forever warm, forever counterfeit tone.

There ought to be a law: a truth in lending (your heart) disclosure?

Again he felt a pang of sorrow. Some mish-mash of guilt and remorse that was inextricably connected with her. Gail's anguish was her second skin; if she could she probably would have shed it.

RAND'S MONOMANIA—this time, in the form of his latest amour, a girl called Catherine who was bored beyond redemption by her job in the couturier's shop in Stamford—knew no bounds.

They met over brisket. Brisket! Victor strutted up and down the tiny sidewalk, peering at shop windows, at storefronts heavy with boxed chocolates, lingerie and toddler wear.

"Come here often?" Victor asked.

Catherine passed the test: she did not flinch. She did not grimace. All she did was hand him her card.

Later, over burgers, Rand messed with her head.

Rand moved in for the kill. God but he was good at this!

"Catherine, there's something you need to know. I am a champion in bed."

Catherine sighed. "Really." She scraped cheddar from the burger's face. "How original!"

Chapter 49

This Is It

THE DOC SLIPPED Rand some pills. The doc had a heart. Victor declined the priest, the tube, even the savory distraction of hot Chinese food.

Rand did however accept the pills. Soon enough he slipped into reverie.

The not so comforting mind games that play themselves out right before the fall of the ax.

The doc—Deutsche—was a jerk. Humanitarian? Forget it! In a fit of cruelty—Rand must have reminded him of someone, someone he had once loved, lost or despised—the doctor gave him a handful of speed. Little comfort there. So Rand turned to bliss. Heavenly visions of the stunning, fragrant loving girls of his life.

The hair. The skin, the eyes. At age eight Rand was already smitten. Face it, Vic: you've been in love from the day you were born. Rand's world was a world of love. The bugs, the mealy worms, even Boot's night crawlers, writhed in nonstop tarantella, in fits and starts of desire. Desire reigned supreme—everywhere! This time next year—absent Rand—there'd be another luscious crop of women, not for him but for some other fool's delight.

So many girls. There had been months, entire years, when he barely noticed. Exceptional months. Rand had devoted decades celebrating the dance of life…with stroke books, with the furtive strokes of one hand. Debra. Jane. Anita. Helen!. They were children, mere children, fantasy babes in arms. They gave Victor reason to live.

One time a friend's older sister came on to him. Rand was twelve years old. She pressed her body, a flying carpet, a bed of nails, tightly against him, sealing the moment with a deep 'French' kiss. Another girl clutched his hand all night long in a freezing cabin in Vermont—only that far. Falling in love was the rocket fuel that got him here. His heart was shattered. Rand tried his best to think about sex, not Thomas Edison. Sex, not death row.

"Any last request?"

"As a matter of fact, sir, I do. I'm writing a book. About all the girls in my life."

"No good," said the warden. "We ain't got all day."

Fear had a smell and so did lust. Could they round up a Buddhist priest? After all, he was a big fan of heaven. And an even bigger fan of cunt.

Chapter 50

Gail Rachel Revived

When she awoke from the chemical bath everyone's first thought was safety. Rescue. Medical viability...all stuff like that.

Gail Pomerantz was fine, though. Intact in body, spirit and mind. (Later on, of course, Rand came to question exactly how intact.)

Vic had his nanobiology texts carted away. The waste management company was kind, even gracious. The guys would do anything for a buck.

The first few weeks all she wanted was the shower. Good hot showers, and plenty of them. Rand soon lost track of the number of midnight expeditions for body wash, pomades, gels, lotions, potions, female products not meant for the eyes of any man.

Anything to add fragrance to the Amazon rain forest, of Gail's splendid perpetual bath. She was hungry—voracious—most all the time. Voracious: wieners, rashers of bacon, beef jerky by the dozen. At first she was terrified at the prospect of sleep. Understandable. She had slept enough.

"I want jerky," she said.

This was deeply puzzling to Rand. The meat locker was filled with the stuff.

"We have jerky, my pet. As much as you want."

"No!" she stormed. "I want squirrel jerky," she insisted. "I want you off your fat ass, I want you on your knees at dawn, hunting in the woods…and don't bother coming home till you've bagged at least a dozen. Then you'll cure them. You'll hang them up to dry."

"As long as I'm going out…anything else, dear? See, I know why I am here, why I am on this life journey. I am here to please you, to please you as much as I am humanly capable. Your wish is my command!"

Gail *née* Pomerantz held her engagement ring up to the light. She enjoyed the play of color upon its seemingly infinite facets.

She pulled a brush through her hair. She wasn't ready to traipse about naked, not yet anyway. Terry cloth would do fine. The terry robes were a regular feature in their lives. She had flashbacks. Over breakfast, Gail Rachel muttered inaudible, mostly incoherent remarks about nitro tanks.

The wedding would be huge.

RAND paid a visit to the local Mormon fellowship. Due diligence, he told himself. The young men in shirtsleeves were always helpful, reliably and perfectly polite.

"Can I find my family tree?"

"Certainly," the young man said.

They were happy to help. First you found the tree, then you grafted yourself, your issue, and your forebears to the huge arboretum of the Church of Latter Day Saints. Missionary work with a smile.

"The name, sir?"

Meantime, Rand's attention had wandered to the larger than life sized frieze on the opposite wall: a smiling sci-fi Christ, sharing Thanksgiving fixings with the joyous Native Americans of Plymouth Rock, New Amsterdam, Manhattoe…

"Pomerantz. Gail Pomerantz." Gail insisted on keeping her surname. Rand was on a mission: find out from which stunted family tree it had dropped. Which snow-blasted tundra had given rise to her and her dog-faced kin?

The lad grimaced. That was a bad sign.

"Funny kind of name, sir, don't you think?"

Rand glared at the zealot. "I married it."

"Sorry, sir. More's the pity." The light coming off the boy's starched shirt sleeves…suddenly caused Victor pain.

"Tell you what, sir. I need to get with my supervisor. Not to worry: we will get this puppy solved!"

The supervisor, barely older than the trainee, though more pinkly complected, ambled over with the confidence of The Redeemed. The co-religionists chatted briefly, *sotto voce*. Rand made out several hushed references to the hotly contested name.

The supervisor offered Rand a seat.

"My friend," he began, "your soul is a star. My soul is a star. I would like to invite you and your beloved wife to join our heavenly family."

"And the bad news—?"

"The bad news, sir, is that there is no such name. Our brotherhood keeps a vast storehouse of names, stored on mainframes miles beneath the mountains. Pomerantz is most definitely not one of those names."

He watched Rand closely. "Sorry."

"Me too." Worse still, the marriage would go on.

GAIL was great. Honey take out the garbage. Honey do the dishes. Bring in the paper. Do the laundry. Jump off the Tappan Zee. Don't forget the neighbors. The furnace. The heat. Vacuum everything. Feed the pony. Kill the grasshoppers. Invite the alderman over for a drink. Pluck the dandelion. Paint the house. Go to work. Watch TV. Stay on the straight and narrow. Ask for help. Take a bath. Don't play with yourself. Do the shopping. Vote. Pay. Pay. Pay. And while you're at it, don't forget to breath! Show enthusiasm. No point in having a family if you can't enjoy it. Smile. Be kind to animals. Eat animals. Don't eat animals. Everything in moderation. Put away your clothes. Have some juice.

Chapter 51

Rand Regrets

VICTOR'S TIME AT THE AGENCY weighed heavy on his hands.

Gail's family was small but extended. Her brother was a bag man for the mob.

MORRIS, scion of an insurance family, trustee of an inheritance that he refused to discuss, was with Norma and Bernice. At the moment Bernice—who spent the greater part of her day in curlers, having her fingernails cropped stiletto-style by a squadron of happy Vietnamese girls—was in social limbo, inhabiting a twilight zone somewhere between suburbia and hell. In the guise of true friendship, Norma and Stan insisted that Vic meet Bernice. Sweet of them but irrelevant. Irrelevant because Vic was preoccupied at the moment—obsessed would be more accurate—with Gail Rachel. They foisted a chalky Chilean wine on him and then of course expected him to talk.

Vic eyed the bottle covetously. Only an inch stood between him and raving madness. Not enough to dash his inhibitions, certainly not enough to toss him head first over the not insignificant conversational hurdle.

"Let's pry, eh?" Vic said.

"That bad, love?" Norma shifted her rayon-clad buttocks

across the plasticized seat. It if weren't for the swollen ankles and the occasional neurologic lapse, Norma might have been a contender.

"No more wine, thank you," Vic said. She could keep the Monterey Jack too.

"Guys, guys, guys…the piteous plight of the captive audience. Sure you want to hear this?"

Norma and Morris locked a conjugal gaze on poor hapless Vic.

"What could be so bad? In my book, Gail is a nice girl. Maybe even the right girl."

"Morris!" his wife remonstrated. "Shame on you! Let the man speak."

Victor Rand stood. This shit was too heavy, even among friends. He started to speak with his hands.

The hands gesticulated, conducting arcs of nascent meaning from Victor's mouth, fingertips, gullet. "You're God, God in heaven, right? Except you're having this really bad day. So, God, you get this really mean look on. Nasty little thunderbolts, torrential tsunamis, fly like popcorn from the warped concession stand of our heavenly Father. Flash flood in Topeka: goodbye, orphanage. Train wreck in Spokane: so much for the jejune soccer team. Too bad! But the Lord still isn't satisfied. There will be hell to pay. That's why he created Gail."

"Gail Rachel. Something Old Testament, something biblical going on there, wouldn't you say? Gail almost checks out—her car gets broadsided by a drunken motorist—but Hashem has bigger plans for her. No, to spite us all, Gail lives."

"And goes on to marry Victor," Bernice interjects.

"She metes out the wrath of the Lord. And please don't interrupt."

"Sorry, dude," Morris says. "Gail Rachel insists on a house by the shore: down the shore, as they say.

"A stone's throw from the in-laws, who are ready, willing and waiting, poised at any and every moment to visit. Come visit... Vic considers a whole body condom—but doesn't know where they are sold.

"Gail, in case you didn't know, is a terrible person. At first Vic doesn't know. There will be kids to raise, nannies to charm, play dates to ponder."

Finally Morris gets it.

"A regular putsch-and-a-half for our friend here," Morris observes. "A real deal—a real ordeal."

"Then she starts with the insomnia. Not that she can't sleep. More that she is physically addicted—in this case, to violent television news."

"Welcome to America!" Morris says.

"Tuesday night cat-fights," Vic explains. "Sex shows, Larry King, Tony Soprano... We're talking Cablevision, man."

Nu?

"GAIL RACHEL up nights with the box. Cablevision, obscene acts and language, televised catastrophes of every stripe."

"Where are you during all this?"

"I could be anywhere... scouring the city for all night pharmacies... in hot pursuit of moisturizers at three a.m. But wait: it gets better..."

Maybe Morris had some Goldschlager. Rand could ply them with drinks. How else could they go on listening to this drivel?

"We started out as city folk, yuppies straight out of Anne Beattie, Maeve Binchy, *The New Yorker.* You know the drill. Down the shore came later. When we hit the shore, well that's when things really spun out of control."

Fire engines, klaxons, ambulances screamed by. A three alarm blaze. But all that was cavernous silence compared to the noise in Victor's head.

"Enter the sandwich generation. Gail's dad was almost killed in a car accident (ironic, no?). And her mother had, as they say, a cancer.

"Gail wigged out. Melt down! She became emphatic, to an extreme. Explicit to the point of lunacy. 'Vic,' she says, 'your needs come last."

"Hey brother," Morris says, "that's called marriage. In sickness and in health—"

"Not in my religion," Vic says.

"So Gail survives a near-fatal brush with death only to foist an even worse fate on you."

Vic isn't sure he cares for his tone.

"Don't pretend you understand."

"He doesn't have to understand," Bernice says. "What matters is that he cares."

"Weekend after weekend driving nowhere, our eyes and arms and hearts open to the majesty of central New Jersey. Shangri-la. Camelot! Gail Rachel riding shotgun. Gail Rachel weeping or blaming. Or both. The city, the galleries, all the things we loved, were gone, she said, gone forever. Needless to say, it was all my fault."

"Obviously."

Vic continues. "She went to dinner with her yoga instructor."

Morris didn't have to ask.

"No doubt a hunk, a boy toy. Am I wrong?"

Norma returns. Vic thinks her nose is bleeding but at a time like this who really cared?

"I would not have made an issue out of it."

"Gail made an issue out of it."

"Pardon me. It?"

"That she had the right to have friends. To befriend anyone she chose—whether yoga instructor, janitor, or stevedore, each with an eye on her ass."

"What else did she say?" Bernice asks.

"It's not like I fucked him or anything."

"So what was the harm?"

CHAPTER 52

SADNESS. GOD. SEDUCED AND ABANDONED

IT STARTED WHEN HE WAS BORN, feeling that he was anomalous. Life was tough. Or so he told himself when he needed consolation and despair.

The rejection thing was a bitch and a half.

College: a new start. Away from home…Rand ran with the pack. The hipsters were smoking hash, dropping acid, or doing agitprop. In the name of progressive labor, peace, pot, and pussy.

Rand ditched his first girl—she liked him too much. Also, she was way too beautiful, way too available. The way she spread for him, the reality of her body, the miracle of her breasts, her golden close-cropped triangle—devastating. completely blowing him away. Debbie was patient, too. Was it the hashish, his nerves, or the riddle of her acceptance that drove him away? Rand was scared to death. That's why they kept at it, lungful after lungful, all night long. Finally they passed out. With the coming of the dawn, Rand wanked himself to half-mast, he was in! The very next day it hurt when he peed. On his way to infirmary he saw female underthings, rippling on a clothesline in the breeze. An omen. A message. He had transgressed! He had taken on the Goddess; now he and his hubris would pay. His UTI was a harbinger, he was sure, of worse things still to come.

Rejection? Rand knew something about that. At college Rand dropped some acid and challenged God to appear.

'God,' he shrieked, his petulant plea echoing pointlessly off the dumb walls of the dormitory room, 'if you're here—if you're there—if you're fucking anywhere—this would be an excellent time to appear. I'm not asking for much!'

His reasoning, awash in a reading blitz of transcendental philosophy, was this: the LSD would prime his spirit, would sensitize his brain to such a divine pitch that if He (or She or It) existed at all, He (or She or It) would be hard pressed to play mum, to deprive him of the splendor of their Heavenly Being. Was the Creator kind? Would the Creator manifest, giving this poor misguided child a shard of succor, a parent's loving touch, whether physical or mental, or something beyond words? Or was this Creator the cruel covert God of the Hebrews, a shithead divinity who left souls like Rand, numbering in the millions, grasping at straws, marching to the ovens, to become lampshades, piles of gold teeth?

Rand kept at it. Stood on the edge of the bed, raising his fists of fury in despair to heaven above. Rand pleaded implacably, doggedly, ineffectively. He thought: Mayan priests at Chitchenitza. Obsidian knives butterflying pectorals…The martyrs of Masada, holy benedictions on every bleeding lip, hurtling through space to meet their 'beneficent' maker. Rand yelled. Rand implored. Rand's tears boiled down, a baptismal lube job that might grease the skids enough to get The Mofo to talk.

Didn't happen.

The American reader wants more in a book. The reader wants more than iteration, wants more than pathology rehearsed *ad nauseam*. Redundance! The reader loses patience with the same hackneyed tales of jealousy, betrayal and imagined revenge.

The writer too gets stymied, gets his fill. Seduced and abandoned. Getting blown off by chicks is one thing; but abandoned by God??? That was something else.

Chapter 53

The Love of His Life

THE DALAI WOULD COME NEXT. The second child came into our life like a blessing from God. When first he arrived in this world he had the round head and matted down hair of a sweet new thing. His eyes were open and he wore a perpetual smile. The eyes were almost bigger than the face. He came to us with a Phrygian cap. He was all the good things in life. The lying-in cap they gave him was fleecy soft, with blue stripes that circled around. Even his sleep was nectar from the gods. We watched him sleep and purr all through the night. He was smiling, he was so innocent and happy…he was interested in everything. He knew me, I could tell by the way he took my finger. His gums were still absent teeth. Not much later, when he could handle the greater ambiguities of life, life outside the bassinet, he slept between us in our bed. Still he purred. His head had the fragrance of heaven, a kind of oil that is part God and part the fruit of your loins. You kiss the head a thousand times and still it's not enough. The child in his high chair becomes prince of the realm. You know you've seen it all, watching the baby eat sweet peas, carefully, with intention, one pea at a time. The spaghetti ends up on his face; the rest finds its way to the floor. He eats spaghetti strand by strand. Or not, depending on what else is going on at the time. You are so entranced by the innocence of that little heart that you completely forget about time. The book you are writing, the neighbor you hate, the clogged gutters lose their meaning. The bottle hangs from the child's mouth casually, effortlessly: Bogart with a half-smoked butt in his mouth. Look, ma: no hands!

He gets older, older by degrees. You notice the actual passage of time. All he wants is to go on the swing. Fool that you are, you get bored pushing him. He finds a lifelong nemesis—bees—and this amuses you too. He will wear anything provided the sleeves are not too long. His feelings about the dog are complex. He is neither the master nor the puppy. The dog is bigger and stronger, but all that works out fine.

"Da-da," my baby says. Imagine that. Da-da!

THERE IS MORE. My son says, are you a good psychiatrist? Why don't you use psychiatry on mom?

I want to get some handcuffs and handcuff you two together.

Don't get married again you were married twice already.

Will you come to my birthday?

Rand writes it all down.

"LAST NIGHT I'm reading him a book and for the second night in a row he asks, 'How can I go in the book?' He wants to go into the book. I explain that if he closes his eyes and imagines hard, he can go in the book. This isn't good enough cause he asks again, 'How do I go in the book? Get in the car and drive there?' "

THIS MORNING he sees some clothing under the bed and points it out. I ask what he sees. "A lot of clothes?" I ask. "No," he says, "just one clo."

I show him a bank statement—his savings account—and he is overwhelmed by what he sees. $10,000! He says he will use the money to buy great things, like 'great operations', for me.

Chapter 54

Rand and King Sol

Neither rhyme nor reason play a part in King Sol's incarceration. He was a tenant on death row. Or a lifer, perhaps, placed there to amuse the rest.

Rand: I'm going nuts, man. Crazy with sadness, nostalgia. I threw away too much, wasted all those years gone by.

King Sol: Ahh…

Rand: Such as excellent, loving woman…

King Sol: The kind who step out of a Caravaggio, parachuting from heaven right into your arms.

Rand: Do we get a second chance in life?

King Sol: Not you, my friend. Let me tell you about my dream girl. Lenore Machtinger she was called. An albino—an albino *extraordinaire*. Her skin an alabaster membrane. She had long cornsilk hair…

Rand: A *shiksah*.

King Sol: …and shocking pink crisscrossed eyes. A fetching smile… Emperor Tojo glasses too. Shoulder blades sharp as darts. Like dorsal fins, pterodactyl wings…

Rand: Hot damn.

King Sol: Here you go, mate. Today's *News of the World*.

Rand: Ready. Set. Go.

KING SOL: Brad Massa, sergeant general at the munitions dump, was spirited away by the military police. In Baghdad, no less. Weeping copiously, he accepted handcuffs and court martial, muttering 'finger cots for the children…never forget the children.'

KING SOL: In a dung-beetle's heartbeat I carom wildly from hopeful expectation to apathetic indolence, from misanthropic cynicism to grateful spirituality…then abject misery words cannot describe.

RAND: Nothing that Sparky can't fix, eh?

KING SOL: Better talk to Deutsch. Deutsche and his friggin' philology.

RAND: Say what?

KING SOL: I said, The origins of pinochle are to be found in freemasonry.

RAND: Fuck. Gimme that *News of the World.*

Chapter 55

Deutsche Redux

At the very end this is how my friend Hector Deutsch pulled through. Decades of onanistic exertions, amply fueled by pastry and girlie magazines, finally took their toll. Hector's heart had the size and consistency of rotten cheese. Life support? They hooked him up to a dog's heart. The brave little organ, no larger than a child's fist, beat on heroically, did the best it could. Must have been a Chihuahua. Hideous, keeping him alive like that. Feeding him flakes of goldfish food, multi-colored flakes like dandruff scales—salty, noxious and dry.

Deutsche's paper-strewn lagoon stank of coffee, grapefruit rind, and the nail parings of a thousand guilty fingers.

From Deutche's *Prolegomemnon and Apologia, Toward A Universal Chemical Castration:* "Like so many insects, they [we] hurl themselves at each other in copulatory frenzy, desperate to sacrifice their soldier ant selves in the service of propagating the species…"

Chapter 56

A Word from Duchamp

Finally Marcel talked.

"You boys need a pep talk," he said.

"Lose your fear," he said. "In 1994, R. B. Noll reported that he was able to completely cure warts in 6 out of 7 patients who had completely failed all prior treatments. This was spectacular news.

"These dramatic results, documented in the journal *Developmental and Behavioral Philology,* was ignored, was summarily dismissed. Who knows? Given sufficient time, the scientific community argued, the warts might have disappeared on their own.

"Wrong! Studies comparing hypnosis to placebo found significantly greater wart loss among the hypnotized subjects. Wart-bearers treated with placebo (sugar pills, make believe treatment) did better than those who received no treatment at all.

"Voodoo? A field day for ignoramus anthropologists, miserably failing to explain 'voodoo death.' Voudon outcasts, cursed on behalf of the community by the witch doctor, suffered miserably, then died. The belief that one had been cursed invariably led to death.

"The so-called placebo effect may have a physiological basis as well. Experimental dental procedures demonstrate that a robust placebo response (the patient believed she was given a strong narcotic painkiller) is eliminated by drugs that block the brain's endorphin (pleasure) centers. We are hard wired to protect ourselves from disabling pain and anxiety.

"This tells me that something happens with hypnosis, with the power of suggestion, something that affects the body's immune function and our very capacity to feel. 'The power of mind' is no joke. Think your way to health, to a perfect life-partner, to millions. Some people actually do!

"Three pounds of gray matter…the brain…a powerful engine indeed! It's a beautiful thing. Pointed in the right direction it creates worlds of untold beauty and magnificence. Left untended, the mind festers, turns in on itself, wreaks untold havoc."

Electrocution? That's a different kettle of fish…

"Maybe we can transcend war, unhappiness and disease.

"Without going to extremes, it may be possible to take the same awesome energy that can destroys warts—or sculpt a *Pietà*—and use it to lose anxiety. misery, tears.

"Anxiety is pandemic in these troubling times—especially on death row!"

The reaction to terror cascades into destructive physical stress. Body systems go on high alert, resistance to germs takes a nose dive. It becomes much easier to get sick.

"Fear is the weapon. Anxiety and stress are the sad consequences of catastrophe and fear.

"'Right now we have a terrific longing to succumb, to surrender, to live our lives cowering in abject fear. Or through focused action, education, meditation—through higher better love, we can lose those unsightly warts."

Small consolation. The buckles on Sparky's straps shone with a dull all-knowing gleam.

Chapter 57

Putting Out the Dog

RAND HAD BEEN SURPRISED, shocked even, at all the hoopla surrounding the adoption of the dog.

The manager of the facility—a literal manger, a shelter for strays, and animal foundlings—ushered them into a pungent room that served as inoculatorium, weigh station, and sometime administrative office.

The woman herself—as is so often the case with handlers and owners of pets—had taken on the canine features of her furry charges. She was not very friendly. Not friendly at all. Waves of suspicion rolled off her like heat from freshly laid macadam.

She had a grossly broadened nose. The nostrils flared like a dragon's. Copious nostril hair, too. He visualized her with a real leather nose. Her hair, bleached and leonine. put him in mind of an abandoned Quonset hut.

The woman eyed the couple skeptically.

The adoption (if permitted) was strictly provisional: a test run whose outcome was uncertain. About this she was perfectly clear. Had the Rands owned dogs before? Why did they want one now?

Did they have time for a dog? What if the creature—a seven-year old Samoyed—bit their child? What then?

The man's wife, by turns maudlin, lurid, yet radiating a hot effulgence of misanthropy coupled with unimpeachable love, reassured the woman on every count. Following further professions of unstinting commitment, of tender loving care, the customary exchange of signatures, cash, and avowals of selfless devotion took place. At last the dog was theirs.

"YOU'LL TAKE GOOD CARE OF HIM!" the dog lady barked.

Can't say they weren't warned.

His boss said, "Seven year old dog? You're out of your freakin' mind."

Right. Life was tough enough. Why take on added burdens, additional risks? The creature would challenge their suburban way of life; sooner rather than later the dog would reach her golden years, serve them up an ever more costly senescence, replete with an exponentially growing balance sheet freighted red…

Meantime, his life wasn't getting any easier. There were bills to pay, kids underfoot, weekends hijacked by a limitless stretch of car pools, soccer games, T-ball tourneys, shredded to ruin by innumerable athletic contests involving balls, nets, spheres, and all manner of competitive sport. There was a dreariness, a desperation to it all that puzzled him. What would all these people do without their horrible thankless chores?

As predicted, the dog took on countless infirmities with the passage of time.

It would be nice to be able to say there was a gradual wearying, an attrition of substance and spirit presaging the deterioration that followed next.

But this was not the case.

Rather, the deterioration proceeded by quantum leap, in convulsions of damage and decay that were fielded with heroism by this family in need.

One particularly rough winter the creature tumbled on the sheer grade of an ice-glazed step, snapping her Achilles' tendon in the process. Perhaps that incident was the harbinger of all the rest. That incident was the beginning of the end.

The fall cost the dog two months in a webbed sling, the limb tightly and brightly bandaged in shocking pink gauze. The bandage was harrowing to the eyes, to the soul, to Rand's wallet.

Then there were the Elizabethan collars, tincture for the beast's eyes, for sores, poultices to rid her of fleas, infestations and maladies that to Rand seemed specious, capricious. Rand rankled at the thyroid storms; the miserable jaundices that came and went; the dog syphilides; and then of course there was the endless round of obscure endocrine disorders, adrenal masses, swollen glands and lymphatics both known and uncharted... Rand took umbrage at the leakages, spillages, compound fractures, skeletal hits and misses, parasitic incursions, veterinary inveiglements, canine specifics and nostrums, kidney stoppages, gastric flux and reflux...the emesis, encopresis, enuresis: suffering of satanic proportion, all the suffering to which incarnate spirit is heir...suffering cured by nothing, going nowhere fast...dog dermatoses; supernumerary nipples; canine trench mouth; swine and bovine flu; parasites and protozoons; ossifications; osteoporoses; eradicable carcinomas; sarcomas; moxebustions; and aromatic evil-smelling specifics...

ONE DAY at table Gail Rachel was serving kohlrabi and veal chop, just the way he liked. His wife cast a silencing glance at the boys, grew stern. A pall descended on the room. The only audible sound was that of the dog, struggling heroically to lick up a little pond of chocolate milk that had spilled off the table.

"Honey, we need to talk," she said. Her tone gave it away. Whenever she got like this his stomach gave little flips.

He choked on a last mouthful of kohlrabi, tried to clear his throat.

"What?"

She looked at the children, took a deep breath as though she were about to dive, and finally spelled it out.

"It's something we've known about for a long time."

"Go on." He set the horseradish sauce down. He had a feeling that his appetite was going south.

"It's time, dear."

He wasn't sure what she meant.

'It's time to put the poor animal to sleep."

Right…no problem there. No argument on that score. In fact, he couldn't agree more. The mounting pile of veterinary bills, the thousand and one miseries the sickly hound had to endure, day in, day out…

Gail pushed back her chair and looked with grim determination at her watch. She sighed.

"Now's as good a time as any, I suppose."

The boys—were they laughing or crying? Rand couldn't tell—came over. Each gave him a hug.

"C'mon honey," his wife purred. "It's better this way."

And so they led him out to the car.

CHAPTER 58

NEVEREST

I WASN'T CHASING HAPPINESS. Don't ask me why. All I know is that after 14 years—a cup of warm juice starting my day—I was ready to move on. Not happiness; not exactly misery; was it mastery I sought? A paved road on the left? I habitually chose the rocky road on the right.

That's how it was. That's why I found myself on a wind-blasted tor, not three miles from the naked summit of K2. A fierce gale from the southeast was whipping up. More often than not, these meteorological convulsions came as a surprise—out of thin air. The Gortex, the spun aluminum costumes actually worsened the chill: one had the illusion of wearing protective garments, yet the tramontaine pierced right through the filament-thin duds, made a joke of our flimsy efforts to retain body heat. So much for Eastern Mountain Sports! Those parkas might look fine in Stamford, on Houston Street...they even held up during the wintry city freeze. The frozen and presumably lifeless form of my closest companion, Dr. Shapiro (still harnessed to the daisy chain) hung suspended, no longer flailing, soon to be lost in the empyrean vastness below. Hanging off the edge of the world, flaunting pastel-colored synthetics at 90 degrees below; this mistral was no walk in the park.

Two thirds of my right leg was numb.. Hey: less pain for me! Ice pellets the size of golf balls shot us mercilessly—a terrible cannonade, dinging my facemask when I most needed to see. I could dimly make Shapiro out, his body twisting and turning at every whim of the storm. Shaprio spun about, a limp lifeless rag doll, every now and then taking a terrible collision against the side of the indifferent wall.

A wall of ice. With my one good leg, I attempted to gain purchase, tried to pierce the frozen fundament with the steely crampon's tip. Each kick threatened to loose me wholesale down into the vastness below. Finally I chipped away enough of the icy blue membrane to lodge my boot—no more than an inch—into the frozen rock. My butt, most precariously exposed, hurt like hell. The ass cheeks had long since adhered, an icicle dildo sandwiching my hams, aggravating my already precarious situation.

That was how things stood: a permafrosted leg, an unsteady toehold on the rock face, a rip-roaring ice storm—and two hands with nothing else to do. Directly above, the escarpment was worse than sheer: the igneous vein ran convex, obtuse, jutting wildly out into space. Any attempt to gain a few more precious feet was laughable. A joke. I was not thinking clearly. I was far too scared. Watching Shapiro dangling helplessly like that from the Himalayan yardarm, I knew my time was up. I was going to die.

I groped behind me, hoping against hope that I might reach my backpack. The nylon snapped at my stiffened fingers. At last I had it: the phone. My only contact with the world.

Flipping the headset open, I stabbed a gloved finger the best I could at the first encoded number: home.

How strange, I thought. There I was in a free-fall toward

doom, with all the useless advantages of wireless technology at my frozen fingertips.

I pressed the tiny speaker against my ear. I heard it ring. Permafrost, frostbite and all, it rang once again. There was a burst of static. From the other side of the planet I heard my wife pick up the phone.

"Hello?"

I heard my children yelling, shouting, the lovely human sound of their voices reviving me for a moment. For an instant I forget about my plight. Somewhere in the world my boys were cavorting, besides themselves with glee.

"Gail?" I couldn't believe we had connected. "It's me."

Stunned silence. "I thought I told you not to call."

A hailstone (or was it a crumbling piece of mountain, a precursor of the avalanche surely headed our way) ricocheted off my gelid brow.

"It's me!" I yelled. "I'm hanging off a cliff. K2: perhaps you've heard of it?"

"This is it, babe," I shrieked. "It's my last call! I chose to call you."

"I suppose it's a convenient time for you," she snarled. "Do you ever think of anyone else but yourself? The boys are going wild. Got to go." She didn't hang up, so I pressed on.

"Gail," I pleaded, "I'm in Nepal. Half the expedition dead. Shapiro too. Shapiro's dangling in space…"

She cut me off.

"Everyone knows about you, you and your narcissistic games," she hissed. "And I suppose this is one of them."

I could not believe my ears.

"Can you hang on for a minute?" A conciliatory tone had crept into her voice. "I'm on another call."

No problem! In the near distance I heard a whooshing sound. The avalanche? Why not?

The jet stream forced my head away from the phone. Only two LED chevrons remained lit on the indicator. I was running out of juice. Now I was really fucked.

"Honey," I said. "Still there?"

"I'm back," she said. One of the boys whistled. The other said, "Hi Dad. Don't forget: bring me back a present!"

"What do you want?" she demanded. "What is there left to talk about?"

I was stunned. The miles-deep abyss had to be better than this.

"Call again and I'll alert the police. I'll call Interpol. I'll have an order of protection on you so fast your head will spin."

"Listen," I insisted, "this is the call of a condemned man. You are the last person on earth I can talk to. I love you."

I meant it.

She didn't care.

"Well I don't love you," she said. "Call somebody else."

"I can't believe you're saying that."

"What's not to believe?"

A sudden gust smacked Shapiro against the wall. The sound of the body hitting granite reverberated down the terrible canyon. Looking past his suspended corpse, obscenely dangling there, I made out two other dots below. Like ants, crushed blackberries., currants. These would be the laggards, the pitiful remainder of our wretched expeditionary group. I held my gaze as long as possible. Neither currant moved against the field of white.

"Okay, got to go," she said. "My mother's on the other line."

My words cracked and crumbled in my throat.

"Can you tell her it's—important?" I croaked. A voluptuous bellowing, as of thunder, reached the crevasse. Now all hell was breaking loose. Bit by bit the ice and snow above us were taking on hallucinatory shapes. Shards and bits and pieces of frozen matter flew past like hoar frost rockets.

"Avalanche," I said. "Tell my sons how much I love them. I'm sorry things didn't work out."

She remained stone deaf to the contrition in my words.

"Look," she insisted, "I'm trying to save on the phone bill. If I hang up on my mom, I'll just have to call her back."

I was silent.

"Go away," she said. "Just leave us alone."

Chapter 59

Mad Captain Rand

What goes around comes around.

With another turn of the dial, in another lifetime, Victor Rand found himself piloting a wreck of a ship. Rand recorded his exploits in the ship's log.

Fear ran amok, like a scourge raining lashes upon the naked backs of the crew. The merciless waves rolled over the mizzenmast, one titanic deluge after another, pounding the deck without surcease.

We were fishers of souls, a parchment trawler, thirteen hundred or so leagues south of the Cape, sailing an indeterminate latitude somewhere east of the Hellespont. The crew—my Great Dane Rollo, and our pilot (also named Rollo)—failed to take heart, failed to bear up under the mighty strain of the storm, despite my boldest imprecations and threats.

"The captain is mad!" I heard Rollo (human) mutter *sotto voce*, looking about him ruefully as though to fend off an imminent blow. The poor wretch applied the rotten stumps of his arms to the deck, fitfully attempting to gain better visual purchase on the typhoon. Years before he had sacrificed the lower half of his body to the hungry jaws of an eel. What remained of him was now consigned by fate, married by necessity, to a tiny wooden platform on casters. The miserable affair served at once as phaeton, toilet, and house of prayer.

The hound bellowed at the maelstrom. Meantime, I labored at the net, heavily weighted down by the day's catch. Straining against the combined fury of the sea, the sickening pitch and yaw of the boat, and my ever-present rage, at last I succeeded in dragging the soggy manuscripts up over the side onto the ship's glistening boards. Was it hallucination, or did I imagine Neptune's wrath abating, the fierce wind and bloodshot sky clearing, replacing the watery Armageddon tossing us will-ye nill-ye only moments before?

I threw open the net and surveyed the day's catch.

The first dripping manuscript was some kind of history. Bound in vellum but (now) smeared, dripping its ragamuffin ink, the book's words ran into each other, forming a meaningless slurry of lines, clouds, and hyphens that lead us nowhere.

The dog insinuated his snout among the volumes, making to fetch and very likely tear the leaves of what was perhaps the handsomest book of the lot. Little Rollo reared back on his dolly, stabbing at the beast with his ugly limb.

'Give it here!' I roared, pulling the volume from the hound's drooling mouth.

Now this was more like it….tenderly, with an artisan's loving care, I traced the next text with a trembling, tobacco-ruined finger. But instantly I was overcome with rage and tossed the unread text back into its watery grave.

Could have been a keeper. Now we would never know. Suddenly the ship rocked, the sky blotted out by the grievous cataract.

I glared at my pilot; left unabused he would have tarried still longer at our haul.

"Take the wheel!" I cried, catapulting him toward the fo'castle with a vicious kick at his miserable conveyance. He shot off in that direction, a gobbet of haemolymph marking his sorry wake…

WE AWOKE to a rosy fingered dawn.

I took a breakfast of rotted kipper. Rollo, already drunk as a lark, watched with imbecilic complacency as the cruel sun broke through the clouds. A single comment from that misshapen lout—even the biscuits he served were alive, maggot-ridden—would have earned him a hasty upbraiding. I stood by my word. I was fully prepared to keelhaul him—the entire crew, for that matter—over the slightest infraction.

He asked for sex but I turned him down. I would have none. There was work to be done.

"The nets, man, mind the nets!" I cried. In a heartbeat I would have tossed Rollo the mastiff overboard but for the distraction of yet another monsoon gathering its wooly head.

"Damn yer eyes!" I squealed, and with one hand lifted the beast (dog) by the pitiful scruff of its mange-worn neck; with the other I tossed the nets, gnarled and knotted beyond repair, into the briny drink.

The roiling waters bubbled black, like the vast eructation of some behemoth. Neptune himself was calling but we withstood the blast, watching instead as the coils of hemp suddenly arced skyward.

Books. Always more books. As though to vindicate himself—to regain his captain's love—Rollo made to grab at the quarry.

"Careful!" I shrieked…I shuddered at the vision of his scorbutic flesh polluting the precious parchments wrested from their long watery sleep.

"Stand back!"

At once he was obedient, fearing I suppose ever more severe reproofs, further imprecations. (Always more where those came from!) I held my tongue, dropped the animal into a bacteraemic puddle, salvaged the dripping wet catch. It was like struggling with a demon horde...but somehow I brought the limp reading matter en masse over the gunnel and from there on to the deck.

Both Rollos mewled.

"What have we here?" I wondered, poking a cadaveric finger (stiffened with pellagra and by misuse) among the sodden leaves.

A treatise, a broadside, a chapbook...of ancient origin, perhaps...and likely to fetch a handsome price at any port of call.

"Yes, yes" I screamed in delight, "this is rare stuff indeed!" I already saw the doubloons the pages would fetch at any world bazaar.

The ship's mascot (Rollo, quadruped) mewled again, a gleaming rope of dog snot listing from his snout. The wretched beast would have charged the still bubbling catch—would have torn its leaves asunder—had not a sudden majestic plume tossed the ship several leagues aloft. For one awful moment, the trawler—worm eaten planks, frayed rigging, death's head quarto, octavo flags and all—hung transfixed in mid-air, starboard garishly lit by the inconstant rays of the sea-choked sun. We might have continued thus, cooked and writhing on Neptune's trident, but for the equally sudden calming of the swell. The boat took it hard, was practically destroyed, plummeting to the water's iron hard surface with a dreadful wallop. Just as well that the yardarm and mizzenmast chose that moment to snap. I gave as good as I got, however, roaring a mighty oath that signaled my determination, my complete and utter willingness to go down fighting.

No matter. Another dripping manifesto, rescued from eternity, clung to my much maligned hand. Were there no living creatures among the deep, none to be brought to the surface by our nets?

Rollo (former biped) now took up a hideous lament, a kind of sailors' chant he had picked up (along with several incurable venereal diseases) along the Malabar coast.

This 'tune', this infernal oraison, this string of barbarous names set to music—music such as only a dying man is capable of—put me in mind of the octoroon whom I had confined several weeks before to the ship's brig (a black hole, a cramped and airless hold that served variously as rat hotel, dog latrine, and sometime repository of irreducible unwashed things.)

Just then a phalanx of white caps, reinforcements as it were of the advance guard (whose rough and tumble we had barely just survived) took us unawares. I was certain we would go down. I dismissed the octoroon from my thoughts. Finally I would get to hang my cleats, my Playboy centerfolds, in Davey Jones' locker... my thoughts a waking dream of meat—glorious platters of grilled meats, savory meats, hams fresh killed, pickled, cured...

Some Leviathan—a sea serpent?—sprung upon the hapless mariners like some fresh spawn from hell, bursting up and right through the fo'castle, exiting quickly but not without leaving a tidy reminder of its unbidden call. What once had been a deck was now a crater, a pit some two or three yards across, granting us unlimited visual purchase on the boiling sea below. This time I walloped both Rollos, holding them over the cracked and splintered precipice until they had something for me. Rollo spat, swore, would have tumbled into the drink...but at last he caught at something and I pulled his stinking carcass back on board.

"A plague on you," I bellowed, "may your pox give birth to devils! What have you there?"

The stupefied sailor—he would have been happier spending his remaining days in the clean glare of some chirurgical amphitheatre, garnering the attention of chloroform-wielding, trepanning medical clerks—held out a sodden mass of pages and barnacle-encrusted leather.

What infestation of words, what scribbler's leavings (I dimly made out *'by...A. Kinsey'*) wrested from the narwhal, from the vomitus of the heaving cetacean, had we come by now?

> The failure of a female to reach orgasm in her marital coitus may be a considerable source of marital discord...The data indicate that among the females in our sample who had never experienced orgasm prior to marriage, 44 per cent had completely failed to reach orgasm in their first year of marital coitus. On the other hand, among those who had a fair amount of orgasmic experience prior to marriage, only 13 per cent had failed to reach orgasm in that first year of marriage. This is a difference of considerable magnitude. Differences which lay in the same direction were apparent in the later years, and even for fifteen years after marriage.

AND what was this, a fragment of an appendix to the earlier volume we had fished from the deep?

In his *Veterinary Metaphysics*, Deutsche champions the notionthat social order among the nutria is infinitely more vexatious and ultimately far more rewarding than its humankind equivalent. In so doing his debt to Brillat-Savarin is obvious. Historical sources strongly suggest that Deutsche spent many hours picking the brains of the latter during a concordat attended by the two in the pubic gardens of the Hague. Nineteenth century Holland provided a unique and fitting locale for this outrageous example of pansyndicalist academic theft.

THIS WAS fine and important stuff. Once again the bonnie sea had gifted us with treasure. We were mired down with nautical nightmares; the dreadnought was collapsing, surrendering itself timber by timber to the unforgiving sea; the deck hands and their captain were quickly succumbing to a catalog of infestations virulent enough to set the entire Sargasso aglow. But I held the wondrous chapbook, this palimpsest from heaven, in the palms of my trembling hands.

SOME have asked why this captain had taken on such soul crushing burthens. Some have crept silently into the captain's quarters to steal a glance at the ship's log, hoping to find some clue regarding the stewardship, the retention on board, of these dubious besotted worthies.

Why, for example, have they not already walked the plank? Flown the gibbet? Trailed the yardarm?

Have I mentioned Rollo's hydrophobia? This single quality touched a chord within my breast. The man's illness was of the galloping, incurable variety. He could be reached by pity, by the caress of a whip or the end of a mop harpooned up his arse—but no human medicine would help. More's the pity that he was trapped in a world of salt water, of brine. Even he knew he could never slake his thirst. This parvenu of pain, this sultan of suffering, should have been scotched decades back…but for the universal appeal of his hydrophobic manias. There was something heroic in the man as he stood before the mast, caterwauling, attempting to balance the astrolabe, to sight and to settle the ever receding horizon along the hills, dales and wretched furrows of his woefully buboed arm. One time, after (again) soiling the astrolabe's lens with carbuncular weepings, I lashed him to the wheel. I hoped I supposed that the arrows of Helios might dry out those festering sores—might burn some sense into that sea-wracked head. Boils, carbuncles, buboes…and here he was with another catch. He extended his syphilitic hand as a peace offering, pilot to captain, on this storm-tossed wreck of a ship.

This was a different kind of catch. A woman—a mermaid, perhaps—struggled among the coils of net. You could not tell where her darkened tresses ended and the coils of seaweed began. Rollo, thoughtless brute that he was, emptied the net's content on the swaying deck. The girl choked, sputtered, then looked up at me with loathing in her aquamarine eyes.

"Fair daughter of Neptune," I began, "by what miracle have you landed here, among us, the lowliest of the low, the scum of the earth, the scavengers of sea-wrack?" My invective did not put her off.

"My name is Gail, sir. Gail Rachel. My father Zach foretold this moment. He said I would find you. I will make you a fine wife, I can promise you that." She made to stand, to shake off

214

the freezing droplets of water that still clung to her naked body like some second skin.

Worthless! Completely worthless, like the seaweed we were forever dredging up. We were fishers of souls, not fetchers of flotsam. I grabbed her by the hair, and with one swift motion tossed the girl and a handful of crappies back into the sea. The roiling water beneath had calmed somewhat, permitting a somewhat more relaxed inspection of the damage to the ship.

Chapter 60

Gail Pomerantz, from the Neighborhood

Her name was Gail.

She was a beauty, from the neighborhood.

One time he was lying sick in bed, thrashing about with fever. She applied a crown of thorns to his brow, leeches to his nipples, then let him rave on. Her love was indiscriminate. (This was long before tie-dye.)

They played a little game to distract him from his woe.

"Darling," she said, "imagine the last words of the guillotined. Among those who could talk, that is."

"Right! My college application essay!"

She dipped the hand towel into the soothing alcohol bath.

"What they said?"

"What who said?"

"The heads. The talking heads."

"They said, FUCK YOU!"

"Did they bray?"

"I wouldn't know."

"The heads in the canvas sack bit at each other—ferociously. Remember telling me that? My favorite bedtime story."

"Hatred that survives the grave."

"A noble last gesture. A parting shot at this miserable world."

“Nothing that a bullet can’t cure.”

“Are you describing an ideal execution, where the shooter gets shot too?”

“Yeah. Right. Gut-shot, too.”

CHAPTER 61

MANNY RADNITZKY

VICTOR RAND HAD A TERRIBLE CHILDHOOD. A childhood sad beyond words. His parents abhorred each other and they let everyone know. There were no limits, no bounds. Victor's father, a fishmonger, stalked the claustrophobic diocese of the tiny apartment as though he might explode. Rand's mother did reliably explode. They were strange, unpredictable, their minds and hearts plucked from the gutter. They did nothing to spare the child the violence and fury of their wrath.

Their single concession to Victor was his name. He was born Manny Radnitzky; he refused to own it. Victor held his breath, refused food until he was so weak that that he passed out in temple. So Victor Rand it was.

The fighting in the Radnitzky house was fierce, something terrible. Victor, ever the solitary, retreated to his *sanctum sanctorum*—his books.

Later in life he would find a series of women who could duplicate, word for word, gesture for gesture, the unwholesome deprecations that Vic's mom had let fly at his dad. Victor buried himself in books.

He could write. He imagined people who actually needed to say things, needed to express what they 'thought.' Any writing

he did from the Radnitzky house was more like war correspondence. Anything more subtle would have to wait.

*Maybe I have something on my mind. Like the need to survive
this house.* At ten he kept a journal. *Even blankness, vacuity,
incomprehension is better than all this.* Writers were a friendless
orphaned breed. *Loneliness*, he wrote, *claims me for its own.* You
want things; you fear things; you avoid things. Just when you
take the first faltering steps toward the object of desire the whole
damn thing comes crashing down.

In 1987 Rand wrote:

He scaled the heights
But lost his grip
He surrendered
To the pull of earth
Mother gravity
Sucking him down down
To the childrens'common grave.

BY 1987 RAND had a solid berth at the agency. He passed among
men like any other. A shadow. He never slept. He made love
to his wife, certain that the codicils of a decent night's sleep had
been completely met. Why couldn't he sleep? Somewhere, on
agency time no doubt, he read about a certain state 'enjoyed' by
spiritual aspirants. A state of enduring consciousness in which
sleep was no longer necessary. On the back of a matchbook ('We
sell delicious sandwiches') Rand wrote, *We rise from the ocean
of being. Someone loans us eyeglasses. The loan is temporary.*

The fog is thereby penetrated, but only by mere inches. This is insomnia. What is it with me? What happens when I batten down the hatch, when I invite sleep to stay for the night? Who decided to dole out this nourishment to me in such sparing portions? Tension, wakefulness, the myriad sounds of night…the sparrows dropping almost silently from trees to their final resting place, the refrigerator achieving its nightly crescendo of motoric sobs…a comfortless infertile and friendless web…

Sleep was only half the issue. The other was being awake. Why was he awake, when all he sought was absolution, revenge—or sleep? A servomechanism, sporting a boutonniere…And then of course the Names, awful names flying at him on reptilian wings, brats from the phylogenetic wasteland…Was he really awake, when the love he knew was septic, tainted, when the love he knew arrived in niggardly aliquots, doled out in droplets from the rusted spigot of a clogged sink…*I cannot love, I cannot choose, I am simply the master of ceremony with boutonniere, egging on the faceless assembly of selves.* There is the occasional rotten tomato, the pie in the face.

Who ordered the blinds? Who was forced Rand's eyes and ears into martyrdom, into a hieratic embrace?

Victor Manny Radnitzky, age 12:

And you'll listen to the wind—
Listen to the wind!
Hear the harpies blow,
Feel the struts and pinions
Those are your heart-strings, snapping!

VICTOR regretted his loneliness. He would throw his body into others but for the risk of disease. He wrote, This is an era when the gradual ingress of a fatal epidemic has rendered sexual escapism a thing of the past. Or a sure recipe for suicide.

Rand at age twelve:

See, I had all this time on my hands: time to think, to weigh, to consider. Time to perfect my role as hapless victim of a never-ending cycle of thought, recrimination and guilt. My sister, three years my junior, cowered with me behind the door as Mom and Dad went at it like limbic heavyweights: his lack of ambition, his unwillingness to take her where and when she wanted to go, etc. I failed my sister. I hoped beyond hope to rescue her, to save her from the dragons and cock-fights at home. We could start a new life...anywhere but there!

Foremost among my thoughts was this longing for the 'absolute.' Mom treated me like hell. Her fury, unleashed, was that of a monsoon at full blast. She would bellow, shriek, set my little heart pounding. That bellowing hurt, made me unloved. She turned me against my dad. I got weeks and months of cold stony silence from him. He came home, sat down to a singleton's supper--never uttering a word. There was anger and hatred aplenty in those absent words, that frozen glare. I longed for what William James described as the feeling of 'oceanic bliss.' The mystic state of union. I longed for the embrace that would return me in one fell swoop, one thundering dissolution of self, soul, and ego, to my pre-organic origins. This devilish desire, this thrust toward the Absolute (and the Absolut, as well), has taken on so many forms, so many avatars. My first short and curlies were barely in before I was a dedicated student of freemasonry, Eliphas Levi, Violet Firth. I was a Rosicrucian, too. This was the family curse. The Radnitzky taint, as it were. It has taken the guise of spiritual quest, outfitted itself in the trappings of frenzied and destructive episodes of auto-intoxication; but mostly it comes to me as a persistent series of images, images of desire, images that parade like a mighty regiment whose main strength grows even as the infrequent healing imago falls by the wayside.

Images? For Rand they are, simply put, SHE. She who must be obeyed. She who will seduce and abandon; She who will ultimately destroy. Lililth, Maya, Kali…Woman as temptress, as destroyer, as dark repository of pleasure and fear. She who holds the key to life and death.

In prison Rand had ample time to reflect on such matters. Soul mate? No such animal. Hell, Gail Rachel was no prize. No creature, no feminine avatar, who could bestow the infinite pleasure Rand so desperately sought. Grace Kelly? Deborah Kerr. June Cleaver?

RAND wrote, *I want someone to devour me. I'll succeed in finding her. But there are no monsters, no hydra-headed Lucretia Borgias, no latter-day Catherines the Great, no Salomes, no Delilahs, stepping from the pages of apocryphal tomes—unless I create them myself.*

His mother, Muriel Radnitzky, kept Rand all to herself. She condemned her husband to a lifetime of loneliness, privation, and despair. Rand's dad was a vagabond, an outsider, an outcast. Rand's mom at once gifted and cursed Rand with infinite atten-

tion, with her version of unconditional love. She was infinitely complicit in Rand's long and frequent absences from school.
Who needed school? Rand reigned supreme, at home in his sick
bed, a true prince of the realm. The comic books, the paperbacks,
the magazines and candy, the television going full tilt... Muriel
taught him to type, she adored him, adored his writing, his draw-
ing. Everything he did was brilliant, worthy of a prize. He would
have a sterling life, of that she was sure. He deserved no less. If
she waged her Thirty Years' War with Rand's dad, so be it; that
was the price of admission to paradise. Rand was destined for
greatness...for great betrayal, too.

WHO AMONG US can truly recall the state of union, the blessed
radiant moments of infancy? Who among us does not yet crave
to be spoiled, cuddled, powdered? In the absence of memory,
we must therefore set out on a vast and arduous task of recon-
struction. Why not admit that one's very first relations were with
good things, things that later poisoned you but which at the time
lacked the obdurate noncompliance of the peopled world? Gradually the joy of being handled, lovingly loved, totally cared for, is
replaced...by what must come to seem like a German industrial
park. The island of surviving spirit sports pennants of pathology.

RAND'S QUESTIONS were legion, innumerable. What of the child
who cannot say, Daddy help me, I'm scared?

In which overbooked arena was I castigated, driven by blows
and jeers and whacks of the cudgel, set against myself in a lifelong algebra of despair? How did I arrive at this zona incerta
of causality, forced up the vertical rock face of this monolith,

only to find myself among the ranks of vacant-eyed ghosts and long-deserted pantheons?

I would if I could deny my tenancy in this empty lonely world.

Wherefore this counting, this idiot's abacus of useless prayer beads and tears? It is as though a terrible wind had risen and scattered before it the colors of creation, tossing to the corners of the earth affinities once alive and elective, the stirring of the blood for concupiscence now gone, sealed forever within someone's idea of a foundry of tin.

IN BETWEEN journal entries, Rand grooms himself, beyond all hope he hopes, in an effort to camouflage the nascent tips of his horns.

Gail, all of you: I advise you to approach this ornate simulacrum, this Chinese puzzle, with great caution. Exert caution, if you will, but tear the bar coded panel off the box, rip the lid from its hinge. Offer up the sixty two million names of God and then look inside!

There you will find a tiny slip of paper…the nucleus of a fortune cookie. It reads, YOU DON'T LOVE ME.

I am simultaneously psychopomp, Hierophant, and Fool.

AT THIS POINT Rand's entries become redundant.

My Life So Far.

Childhood in the Bronx. My grandfather is Dutch Schultz. Or Schmiel. Or Franz Bardon. I don't need anyone else. I got heavily involved in metaphysics, in extravagant fantasies of romance. I work at the human service agency. I will spend the rest of my life trying to fix others.

Appendix

So many lamentations; so little time. Rand read, cogitated, watched *film noir* till it oozed from his ears. The Alchemist's Handbook was filled with recipes for poison. The information was ubiquitous. Rand especially liked the daggers and bullets fashioned of ice—no evidence for the medical examiner.

His friend Matsu, an electrical engineer at an obscure firm in Stanford, showed him what to do. According to Matsu, who doubled as sous sushi chef on alternate weekends, Rand could obtain super high voltage batteries. These dry cells would work fine in customary applications—flashlights, radios, smoke alarms—but when touched, they packed quite a wallop. Drop one of these in salt water and watch the sparks fly!

Hmm. Rand could make nice to her. Play the game one more time, fry Gail Rachel in the bathtub, plead innocent, then book.

He waited for one of Gail's neutral moments. She had been out all day visiting pet cemeteries; this always put her in a receptive mood. She had been brooding, planning for the eventuality of their cockapoo's demise.

"Honey, how's about I draw you a bath?" Rand could not believe his ears. He sounded like Robert Young.

"Nice!" she shouted from the other room. She made some excuse to whomever was on the line. 'Something about a bath,' she explained.

This was working out—even better than he had planned. Rand could add the sal hepatica while she was busy with the phone. The bath salts were odorless, colorless. Rand shook out a half box of the stuff, ran the water hard and steamy, and for good measure lit a candle. Sage and citrus—just what she liked.

"What have I done to deserve this?" she asked.

"Ask no questions, I tell no lies."

"Pinch me. I must be dreaming."

"I'll do better than that." Rand slipped off her blouse, undid her bra, helped her from her chinos. She was enjoying this. Rand felt a twinge.

Gail stepped into the tub. Rand helped ease her in. She lay back, taking a deep breath, luxuriating in this most unusual display of domestic accord.

Rand, still fully clothed, leaned over and kissed her. His hand did a slow walk down her belly till it nestled between her open thighs.

"Mmm…"

"And now for a little surprise."

She reached a dripping hand toward him.

"No, not yet," Rand said.

He slipped the vibrator from his back pocket.

"Ever see one of these?"

"Victor! What on earth…?!"

Rand turned the handle. The hum was low but audible. She pretended to object.

"Victor, you're not actually going to…"

"You know you want it, Gail. Sit back and relax."

"Do I have a choice?"

Talk about rhetorical questions. She opened her legs wider, her feet resting on the sides of the tub. Rand approached with the toy.

THE HEAD of the device—smooth, cylindrical, ergonomic—went right on in. Gail arched her hips forward, up, driving it home. This was it. Drop it in the water, Vic. Just let it go.

Gail screamed. Screamed with pleasure. She clawed at him, wanting more. Gail's writhing turned the bath into a bubbling monsoon. The back of the artificial phallus—by now roundly soaked—inadvertently grazed Rand's hand. The resulting shock sent him reeling. The jolt, sufficient to fell a tree, coursed through Rand's body. He stiffened, convulsed and slammed against the tiled wall.

"You bastard,' Gail hissed. 'Just when I was about to come…"

THE ETHNOPHARMACOLOGIST Wade Davis made a career—and a book and a movie—on the subject of Voodoo death. Earlier generations of sociologists and ethnobotanists lacking the advantages of modern scientific method, explained Voodoo death the best they could. Those marked by the evil eye were doomed outcasts: cursed, apostasized, anathematized, excommunicated. Whatever you called it, it killed you. The *persona non grata* wore his sickness unto death. Then he died.

Nonsense! Poison caused voodoo death. The powdered skin—*Bufo alvarus*, a tropical toad, contained an extremely potent nerve toxin, bufotenin. Micrograms of the stuff killed you dead. The poison was rapidly absorbed through the skin. Micrograms—applied to the sole of the foot, the hand, anywhere—quickly did the job.

Bufotenin paralyzed nerve transmission—instantaneously. Paralyzed the lungs, the heart, the brain.

The boys were at grandma's. The old crone craved the consolation of the young and innocent. Rand would deal with her another time. The powder—covertly obtained by Rand—arrived in a tiny glass ampoule. Rand stretched on three pairs of gloves. A face mask too. The dog could fend for itself. Rand snapped off the tip of the ampoule. filling each hole of the phone's ear piece with several grains of the stuff. Replacing the receiver, he ditched the gloves and left the house. Gail was upstairs, dressing or doing her nails.

Rand called from the car. The phone rang once, twice; at last, she answered.

Suddenly it came to him: *Imbecile*! Gail must not die—her living womb was the unborn Dalai's next port of call.

So it is written.

Fomite
Burlington, VT

A fomite is a medium capable of transmitting infectious organisms from one individual to another.

"The activity of art is based on the capacity of people to be infected by the feelings of others." Tolstoy, *What Is Art?*

Writing a review on Amazon, Good Reads, Shelfari, Library Thing or other social media sites for readers will help the progress of independent publishing. To submit a review, go to the book page on any of the sites and follow the links for reviews. Books from independent presses rely on reader to reader communications.

Visit http://www.fomitepress.com/FOMITE/Our_Books.html for more information or to order any of our books.

As It Is On Earth
Peter M Wheelwright

Dons of Time
Greg Guma

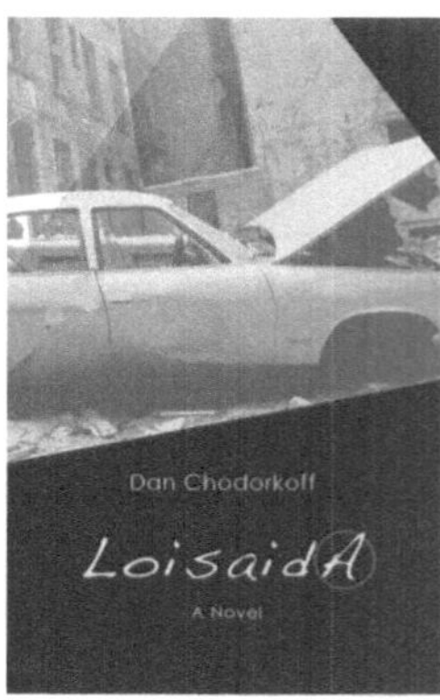

Loisaida
Dan Chodorkoff

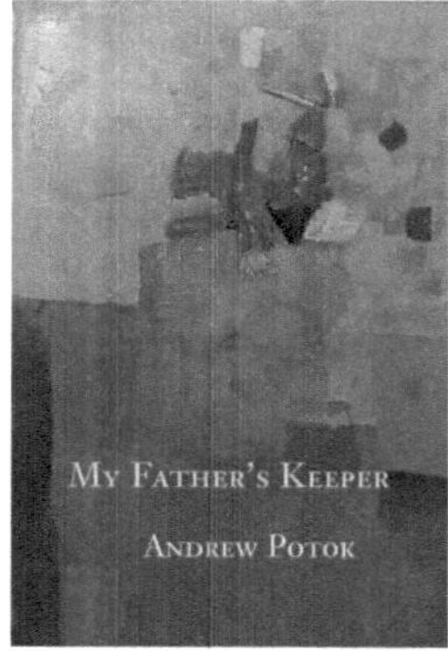

My Father's Keeper
Andrew Potok

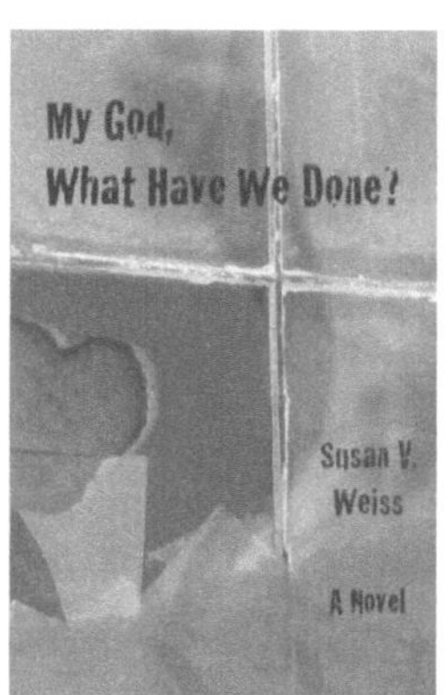

My God, What Have We Done
Susan V Weiss

Rafi's World
Fred Russell

Fomite
Burlington, VT

The Co-Conspirator's Tale
Ron Jacobs

Short Order Frame Up
Ron Jacobs

All the Sinners Saints
Ron Jacobs

Travers' Inferno
L. E. Smith

The Consequence of Gesture
L. E. Smith

Raven or Crow
Joshua Amses

Sinfonia Bulgarica
Zdravka Evtimova

The Good Muslim
of Jackson Heights
Jaysinh Birjépatil

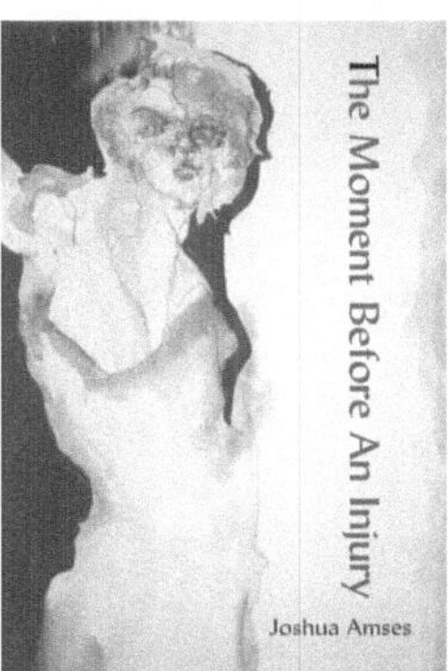

The Moment Before an Injury
Joshua Amses

Fomite
Burlington, VT

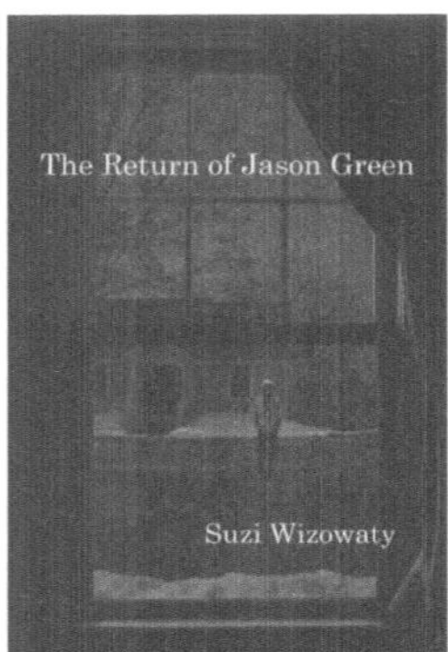

The Return of
Jason Green
Suzi Wizowaty

Victor Rand
David Brizeri

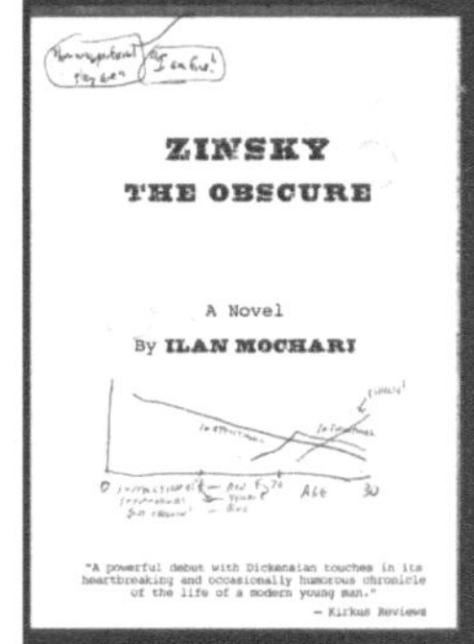

Zinsky the Obscure
Ilan Mochari

Body of Work
Andrei Guruianu

Carts and Other Stories
Zdravka Evtimova

Flight
Jay Boyer

Love's Labours
Jack Pulaski

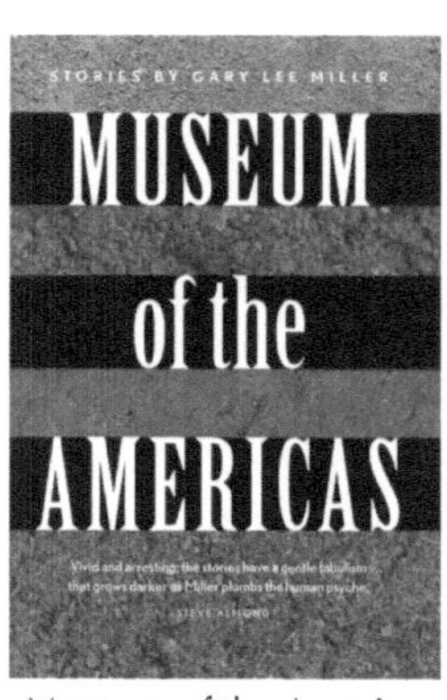

Museum of the Americas
Gary Lee Miller

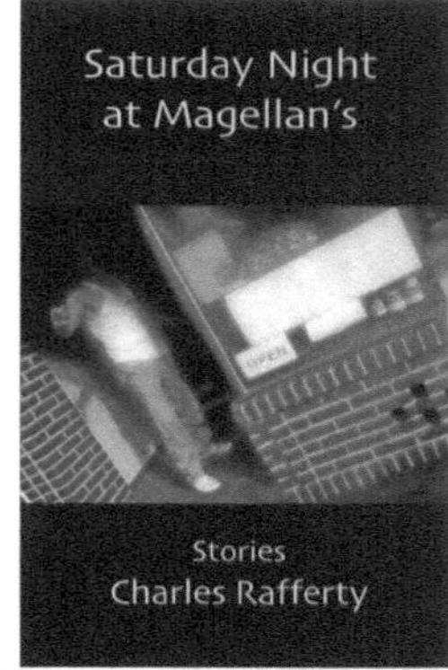

Saturday Night at Magellan's
Charles Rafferty

Fomite
Burlington, VT

Signed Confessions
Tom Walker

Still Time
Michael Cocchiarale

Suite for Three Voices
Derek Furr

Unfinished Stories of Girls
Catherine Zobal Dent

Views Cost E□tra
L□E□Smith

Visiting □ ours
Jennifer Anne Moses

When □ou Remeber
Deir □assin
R□L□Green

Alfabestiaro
Antonello Borra

Cycling in Plato's Cave
David Cavanagh

Fomite
Burlington, VT

AlphaBetaBestiario
Antonello Borra

Entanglements
Tony Magistrale

Everyone Lives □ ere
Sharon Webster

Four□Way Sto□
Sherry Olson

Im□rovisational
Arguments
Anna Faktorovitch

Loosestrife
Greg Delanty

Meanwell
Janice Miller Potter

Roadworthy Creature
Roadworth Craft
□ate Magill

The Derivation of
Cowboys □ Indians
Jose□h D□Reich

Fomite
Burlington, VT

The □ousing Market
Jose□h D□Reich

The Em□ty Notebook
Interrogates Itself
Susan Thomas

The □undred □ard
Dash Man
Barry Goldensohn

The Listener As□ires
to the Condition of Music
Barry Goldensohn

The Way None
of This □ a□□ened
Mike Breiner

Screwed
Ste□hen Goldberg

Planet □as□er
Peter Schumann

My Murder
and Other Local News
David Schein

Picking □ □ the Bodies
James F□Connolly

Fomite
Burlington, VT

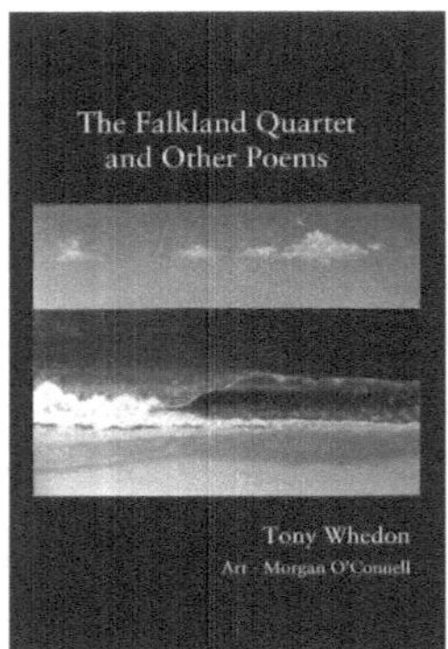

The Falkland ☐ uartet
Tony Whedon